ALIBI II

TERI WOODS

ALIBI II

NARD'S REVENGE

GRAND CENTRAL PUBLISHING

NEW YORK BOSTON

Cover design by Christine Foltzer. Cover art of skyline by Enjoynz/Getty Images.

Grand Central Publishing
Hachette Book Group
237 Park Avenue
New York, NY 10017
www.HachetteBookGroup.com

First print on demand edition: November 2012

Grand Central Publishing is a division of Hachette Book Group, Inc.
The Grand Central Publishing name and logo is a trademark of Hachette Book Group, Inc.

ISBN 978-1-4555-7241-0

ALIBI II

1986

BAMBOOZLED

The State of Pennsylvania v. Bernard Guess
Day One

Nard used all of his man power to contain himself as he sat pensive and breathless, the inside walls of the courtroom spinning emotionlessly. His mind was racing a thousand miles a minute as he saw his life flash in front of him. *No way, this isn't happening. What is she doing? I'll go to jail for the rest of my life.* It was all he could think as he locked his eyes down on the witness, Daisy Mae Fothergill. She was sitting calmly on the stand, nodding ever so slightly as she leaned into the microphone giving answer after answer.

"Ms. Fothergill, you say today that you never saw my client, Bernard Guess, before, is that correct?"

"Yes."

"However, this is your signature, is that correct?" Bobby DeSimone asked as he swiftly walked back over to his table, picked up an investigative report he had marked as Exhibit A.

"Yes," Daisy Mae calmly responded.

"Your Honor, I would like this to be marked as Exhibit A," he said, handing the document over to the judge.

"In this document you state that the defendant was with you on the night in question, is that correct?"

"Yes."

"So, now today you've changed your mind and you want us to believe that you were lying then?" He arched his eyebrows and gaped at her. Then he purposely faced the jury, still waiting for her answer.

"I was paid to say what I said."

"So you can be bought, is that your answer, Ms. Fothergill?"

"Objection, Your Honor, completely inappropriate," said the district attorney as he quickly stood up and faced the court.

"Sustained, watch it, DeSimone!"

"For the record, just one more question, Your Honor?" DeSimone interjected, asking the court's permission in a single breath. He cleared his throat and then began where he had just left off. "Why should we believe you now?"

"I've told the truth here today."

"Are you sure no one paid you, Ms. Fothergill?"

"Objection, Your Honor."

"Sustained."

"No more questions, Your Honor," said DeSimone, strolling over to his chair and seating himself behind the table next to Nard.

Even with DeSimone's tricky and clever line of questioning, Nard's heart continued to sink along with his fate as he bent his head and stared into his lap. *She didn't do it. She didn't give me the alibi.* His eyes were piercing as he pondered choking the daylights out of her. He looked at DeSimone.

I thought she had me covered. Sticks said she had me covered.

What the fuck am I going to do now?

"Will you be re-examining, Mr. Zone?"

"Yes, thank you, Your Honor."

"Ms. Fothergill, you said that you were paid to make the statements you formerly made to the private investigator hired on behalf of the defendant, correct?"

"Yes."

"Did anyone bribe you or pay you today?"

"No."

"The statements that you have made today, you've made of your own free will."

"Yes, that is correct."

"Are you absolutely positive the defendant was not with you on the night in question?"

"I'm positive. He was not with me on the night in question."

"No more questions, Your Honor."

"You may step down, Ms. Fothergill," the judge ordered as Daisy stood up and stepped down three stairs to the floor level of the courtroom.

She glanced at Nard's face. *God, he looks so mad,* she thought as Detective Tommy Delgado and his partner, Merva Ross, took her by the arm and led her out the courtroom.

Inside the courtroom, Nard could be heard screaming at the top of his lungs.

"That's it? She just gets to leave?" said Nard, loudly enough for the entire courtroom to hear.

DeSimone looked over at the jury. Their expressions said a thousand words. Daisy Mae Fothergill had just shot a missile into his battleship, and now, thanks to his client's outburst, it was sinking.

Seated four rows behind Nard and his lawyer, a family was rejoicing and a woman's voice could be heard.

"That's what you get! That's just what you get for killing my brother! You know you was up in that house and you the one that killed him!" the girl shouted, now standing on her feet, ready to jump the four pews and pounce on Nard for the death of her brother, Jeremy Tyler.

"Who the fuck is you talking to?" Nard barked at the girl, ready to jump back at her, her family, and anybody else who had something slick to say out their mouth.

"Counsel, control your client!" ordered Judge Means, banging his gavel on a solid, round wooden plate.

"I'm talking to you. You know you killed my brother," the girl screamed back, tears streaming down her face. Her mother, sister, and two brothers held her back. Her oldest brother, Wink, put his arms around her, holding her firmly to his side.

"Be easy, Leslee. You whylin', man, relax. I'm gonna get the boy, him and his whole fucking family," whispered Wink in his sister's ear as he gripped her by her arm, letting her know to check herself.

"I don't need any more attention drawn to this courtroom." The judge was banging his gavel, calling for order. The jurors were completely caught up in the courtroom soap opera. The entire case was already a fiasco with the media, cameras and news reporters looking for a story to headline the nightly news every day. "Young lady, do I need to have you removed from this court?"

"Naw, we sorry, Your Honor," said her brother Wink as he flagged the judge to continue. "She good, she not gonna say nothing else," he added, as the courtroom turned and looked at Wink and the other members of the Tyler family.

"Any more outbursts made in this court by anyone and you will be removed." Then the judge looked at the jury. "You are to disregard the outbursts and opinions of third parties in this court and the outburst of the defendant as well," he said.

"I can't believe this bitch just hung me," Nard whispered while the judge was still directing the jury.

"Nard, calm down, you don't want to do this, not here, not now!" said DeSimone, looking at him as if he was his father.

"She just hung me!" he hissed through his teeth for DeSimone's ears.

"Look at me!" DeSimone ordered. "I said, not here, not now. You got that, kid? Not now!" DeSimone gripped his shoulders with both hands.

"Get hold of your client, counsel, or I'll remove him indefinitely from the hearing proceedings. Do you understand?" bellowed the judge.

"Yes, Your Honor, I understand," said DeSimone, turning to face the court. He could feel Nard's muscles begin to relax. "Come on, trust me, you gotta trust me."

Nard's mother, Beverly, looked at him. She gave him a look that said, "Knock it off, boy, or so help me God." She had a way of piercing him with her eyes as a look of discontent crossed her face, and no matter how old Nard got, that look always said, "It's about to be your ass," and he calmed himself as his eyes met his mother's. Beverly simply was tired of Nard getting in trouble. It was hard raising him without a father. He had a man in his life, his uncle Ray Ray, who had lived with Nard and Beverly for the past twelve years, but still, here he was in the most unimaginable trouble he could ever be in. And she was there every day in that courtroom with him, fighting for his life. Beverly didn't want to see her son imprisoned like a caged animal. She didn't care what or who, how or when, she wanted her baby home, and deep down inside that was all she was praying for.

"Court is adjourned till tomorrow at nine o'clock in the morning." The judge banged his gavel, the bailiff instructed the courtroom to stand, and the judge removed himself.

Barry Zone, the district attorney prosecuting Nard, simply looked over at DeSimone, smiling like a sly fox at the thought of DeSimone and his criminal-minded client being scolded by the judge. *You should have taken my plea offer when you had the chance. Yeah, you really should have taken that plea.* He couldn't help but think that, and he knew DeSimone had to be thinking the same thing at that very moment. Of course Barry Zone didn't say a word. Instead, he bent his head and pretended to be sorting through his day planner.

Who the fuck does this asshole think he's looking at? DeSimone thought as he looked over to his right at Zone playing with his court documents. He grabbed his briefcase and walked out of the courtroom. *What a day,* he thought as he answered his cell phone. Just as he answered his phone, a voice from behind him called out his name. He heard another person shouting in his direction. And he could also hear his fiancée demanding he respond to her on the other end of his oversized cell phone.

"Excuse me, Mr. DeSimone, one quick question?" said the voluptuous, blonde, and very attractive Gina Davenworth, hustling for her next paycheck as she quickly approached him.

"Hey, DeSimone, your client has no alibi, what do you think his outcome will be?" shouted another reporter from his left.

"Babe, I'll call you right back." DeSimone disconnected the call that Davenworth's voice had interrupted.

"Do you guys mind? That was my girlfriend?" he said as he stared at Gina Davenworth's breasts. If not for that one tiny button on her blouse, her perfect size Cs would pop right out of her shirt and say hello to him personally. As other reporters hovered and pushed one another, Davenworth's body pressed up against Bobby DeSimone's as she closed in on him, her pen and paper still in hand.

"Do you think your client will accept District Attorney Barry Zone's plea in light of today's testimony?" she asked from her soft butter-pink lips as she batted her aquamarine baby blues at him.

"No comment," he huffed at her, rolling his eyes, before busting through the pack of thirsty reporters, out the double glass doors of the courthouse, and onto the courthouse steps. *She wants me,* he thought to himself as he picked up his phone and dialed his fiancée back. He stood on the corner of Thirteenth Street. He looked up at the sky as he heard her answer.

"Hey, babe, I think I just had the worst day of my life. You're not going to believe it. If I don't come up with a master plan, I'm gonna lose. I'm really gonna lose...big, and I never lose, Jo. You know I never lose."

"I know, Bobby, I know," was all she could say. Joanne offered a sympathetic ear and listened carefully to his every word, and she was of course genuinely interested, but Bobby made the final call on everything, including her.

"I've got to get home and go back through this case. There has to be a way to get this kid off, there's got to be."

I SPY

Across from the courthouse in a parking lot sat an old rusty navy blue van with black-tinted windows. Liddles, the owner and driver of the van, sat parked all the way in the back of the lot where no one would pay him any mind. He had a pair of binoculars sitting on the seat next to him, and a McDonald's bag filled with the leftovers and garbage from lunch. The van was thirteen years old, the heat and air were on the brink, and he didn't have a radio. However, he was riding around with a tiny boom box the size of a sneaker box in the backseat, minus the batteries. Liddles had been sitting in the back of the lot inconspicuously for the past five hours, from 10:00 a.m. to 3:12 in the afternoon. He was patient and had been ever since the death of his brother, Poncho. *Don't worry, Poncho, they will all get what they deserve.* Every day he sat parked in the same spot, watching and waiting.

A young woman, dressed casually in a pair of dark brown slacks, lightweight jacket, and a tan button-down blouse, walked across the street and through the parking lot and hopped into the van.

"Damn, my head is itching," she said, pulling the passenger

door closed and taking a brown, curly wig off her head as she began to scratch her scalp. "I don't know how them girls be wearing these things. This damn wig was tearing my head up in that courtroom."

"Put that back on, I don't want you recognized," he said, not wanting to put her in harm's way. "What happened today?"

"Oh, boy, it was a mess in there today," she said, following his instructions and putting the wig back on her head.

"What, what happened?" Liddles asked, as if the two of them were staring at a soap opera.

Karla-Jae, Liddles's little sister, gave him the 411 and lowdown on all the courtroom drama.

"Well, first of all the flower girl didn't give Nard the alibi like she was supposed to."

"What the fuck you mean, she didn't give him the alibi? He's going to jail?"

"Yup, it looks bad," she said, moving the story forward. "No, I swear to God, then some girl jumped up in the back of the courtroom and started screaming at Nard that he killed her brother. It was terrible," the girl said, eyes wider than Betty Boop's and just as serious as a heart attack as she patted her head, which was still itching.

"So, you mean to tell me, the girl said Nard wasn't with her? And some other girl was screaming Nard killed her brother?" asked Liddles, putting two and two together.

"Yup," said Karla-Jae, thinking back to the look on Nard's face before all the commotion. "Nard couldn't believe it. I thought he was going to jump over the table and rip the girl's heart out or something when she got on the stand. You should have seen the look on his face. Nard is bent right now, believe that, real bent."

"Wow," said Liddles, unable to believe a word his sister was saying. He kept trying to fathom the meaning of it all. He just couldn't believe that Nard's alibi had turned stale. "And who was the girl again? The one saying Nard killed her brother?" asked Liddles.

"How would I know?" asked Karla-Jae, frowning at Liddles, not understanding why he was making her sit in the courtroom every day anyway. "Oou, look! There she go, with her crazy family, right there," said Karla-Jae. "Look at him. He was in there, too, right next to her. All of them be in there every day," she said, giving up more information for Liddles to register.

Karla-Jae looked over at her brother, who watched the family through his binoculars, an older woman accompanied by two guys and three young women walking down the steps of the courthouse.

"You know you is crazy, right?" Karla-Jae asked, patting her head, then ruffling her shoulder-length mane, as she swung her hair from side to side, like the girls in the shampoo commercials.

Liddles paid his sister no mind and watched as the family made their way across the street and walked into the parking lot to where the attendant's booth was located. He watched through the binoculars as one of the guys pulled a thick wad of cash out of his front pocket and paid for his ticket. Within a few minutes a gray Oldsmobile was brought to them. He looked at the Pennsylvania tag on the vehicle.

"Kay-Jae, write down this number...PDA-31K," said Liddles as he watched the Oldsmobile turn out of the parking lot. He started the van and followed the car as it turned onto Twelfth Street.

"Where we going?" asked Karla-Jae.

"Write down that tag," he bossed with authority as she

searched the van's middle armrest console for a pen. She did as he told her, just as his oversized cell phone rang.

Wink and his family had no idea they were being followed home. The thought never hit Wink. His mind was too focused on Nard, who was on trial for killing his brother, Jeremy Tyler. Wink and his mother sat in the front of the car while Leslee, Linda, Joan, and Miles had all piled into the back.

"Did you see his face when that girl got up there?" asked Leslee, laughing at Nard.

"God don't like ugly," said Mom Tyler.

"Oh, no, he gonna get his for what he did," said Wink, certain of that. He already had scoped out Nard's mother. He planned on giving Nard a dose of reality. He wanted to let Nard know that he could get at him, through his family, never thinking that someone wanted to get at his.

"He can forget it now," said Mom Tyler. "I don't think that boy stands much of a chance after what happened today. He's going to jail and that's just what he deserves," the woman said as she wiped a tear from her eye.

"Mom, don't cry," said Wink as he slowed the car just a bit, extending his arm and patting his mother's back.

"I'm all right, I just miss my baby," she said, thinking of her second-born child, Jeremy. "I sure do miss my son," she said, wishing her son were still alive and wanting nothing more than to see his killer spend the rest of his life behind bars.

"Look, they turning, fool," said Karla-Jae, pointing at the Oldsmobile turning the corner.

"Damn, why you ain't say nothing?" he fussed back at her, missing the turn the Oldsmobile had just made.

"Let me call you back," said Liddles as he hung up on Cassie, his daughter's mom. He dropped the phone, quickly banged the next right, and tried to double back to see if he could catch them. He couldn't, though, because the car was nowhere in sight.

He looked at his sister as if she were at fault. Liddles was so heated that he had lost the Oldsmobile, he banged the side of his fist down on the steering wheel, causing the horn to blow.

"Don't be mad at me. You the one that can't follow a car that's right in front of you," Karla-Jae said, hoping she could go home now. She had a date with her boyfriend Dalvin and didn't have time to be on no I Spy mission with her brother.

He snatched the piece of paper that had the tag number written down on it out of his sister's hands. He looked at the number, memorizing it.

"I don't know who you snatching from," she said, rolling her eyes and paying him no mind.

He read the tag number to himself once more. His memory tight, he crumpled the tiny piece of paper and threw it out the window. The tag number was sealed in his mind. There was no chance he would forget it. He looked over at his sister and rolled his eyes at her.

Liddles picked up his oversized cell phone and began dialing a number.

"Yo, Reese, your girl still work at the DMV?" asked Liddles as Karla-Jae listened to his one-sided conversation.

"I need her to run this tag for me on the low," Liddles said, repeating the tag number.

"No problem, hip hip," he responded before hanging up the phone. *This is just how simple it is to get at a nigga,* he thought to himself. Before the day was out, he would have an address, and before the night was out, he'd be right on Wink's ass, with his trusty binoculars.

LAW AND ORDER

Tommy Delgado closed the door to the dark blue Chrysler Fifth Avenue sedan. He and Detective Merva Ross stood and watched the car fade away in the distance.

"You think she'll be all right?" Merva asked, digging her hands deep into her jacket pockets, the autumn air feeling brisk.

Tommy stood still, thinking of his partner's question. *Will she?* "I don't know, Ross. But she's been through a lot, that's for damn sure."

"Yeah, she has," agreed Merva as they crossed the street from City Hall and walked down Thirteenth Street. "You gave her a fresh start, though," said Merva as she stopped and looked at Tommy face to face. "You didn't have to fight for her. I wouldn't have. But you did."

Tommy couldn't help but to interrupt his partner. "Excuse me, Ross, you don't fight for anybody," joked Tommy, laughing at his partner, who always played by the book, showing no remorse and very little sympathy for criminals, despite their story, background, or reasons why.

"Yeah, but you did, you fought for Daisy Mae Fothergill, and if it hadn't been for you, she probably wouldn't still be here, and she certainly wouldn't have the opportunity that she has now to start her life all over again. Come on, very few people get a second chance at life. I admire that about you, Delgado, you're all right with me," said Ross, patting Tommy on his back as they walked down the street.

"Yeah, you know, there are a lot of things about me you don't know. I'm just a great guy, an all-around American hero. It's what I do, I save lives," said Tommy, thinking of all the people he really had saved.

"Oh, boy, men just can't take a compliment and say thank you. I should have never said a word."

"Want to grab a bite before heading back to the station?"

"Always that, you gotta ask?" she joked back.

"Snockey's?" he asked, one brow arched.

"Oh, boy, oysters and stewed tomatoes, now you're talking."

Daisy Mae Fothergill had survived the unthinkable. She didn't know how she had managed to get on the witness stand, speak clearly, and answer each and every question presented without breaking down for fear. But she had.

She had seen the look in Nard's eyes. *He was devastated, completely,* she thought to herself. *What could I do? I had no choice.* She reasoned with herself, all the while thinking of the murderer's fate. *He gets whatever happens to him.* She again reasoned with herself. His face had looked like a confused question mark. *He must have really thought I was going to say we were together. He really thought I would listen to Sticks. Why didn't Sticks tell him? He looked at me like he wanted to kill me,* Daisy thought to herself.

It was true, Nard had no idea that Daisy wasn't testifying on his behalf. How could he? He was nothing more than a stranger sitting in the courtroom. But if Nard's looks could kill, she knew she'd be dead. *Please don't ever let him get out of jail,* Daisy thought to herself. She had realized a long time ago how drastic and how serious the situation was when faced with the reality of living a life in police protective custody. The entire fiasco was unbelievable. *How did I even let myself end up in this situation?* Being removed, and built over, wasn't what she had in mind. *At least I got to keep the money from the bank.* Daisy was ready for a "fresh start," as Tommy Delgado called it. He had spent three days and three nights breaking her down, making her agree to testify, after capturing her in Tennessee and bringing her back to Philadelphia.

"Look, what do you want from me?" he had said, taking the last possible pull from his Newport as he smoked the cigarette all the way to the filter before crushing it with his fingers in the ashtray. "I'm giving you a chance to get out of here and make something of your life."

"Who said I need you to give me a chance?"

"Well, maybe I should just send you back out there on the streets and let the wolves that are looking for you tear you apart!" he yelled, frustrated with repeating himself. The way he saw it, testifying was the only chance she had. *What the hell is wrong with this girl? They'll fucking kill her. Is she that stupid that she can't see I'm trying to save her life?*

"Listen, Daisy," said Tommy, as he tried another approach. He took a seat next to her, running his fingers through his hair. He looked at her, then pulled out his pack of cigarettes, lighting another. "These guys you've let yourself get caught up with are very dangerous. Let me tell you, kid, it started with three dead guys sprawled out in an apartment. Then, a young woman and her nine-year-old son were found dead in the same building, believed to be possible witnesses. I got a dead owner of the nightclub where you worked, Daisy, killed for what? Then your landlord is beaten to death. All because of you and this fucking alibi bullshit, and you're gonna be next," he said, drawing on his cigarette.

"How do you know I'll be next?" she retorted, as if he didn't know what he was talking about.

"Why do I even do this shit?" he said, looking at her, before he got up, walked away, and slammed the door behind him.

It would take another pack of cigarettes, two beers, and the help of his girlfriend, FBI Agent Vivian Lang. Of course, Viv would cosign Tommy in a heartbeat. And for Daisy all it actually took was a little foul play to get her to cooperate. Tommy didn't care what he had to do to get her statement and to get her to confess the truth. Besides, it was for Daisy's own good in the end.

"You're gonna fucking testify. Shut up, I tell you what to do. You hear me? You want even more problems, see, I know what you're thinking. I found out about the bank, kiddo. Not good, and guess what, if you don't cooperate, the bank is going to want restitution on that fifty thousand."

"What's that?"

"It's your ass, Daisy. It's that fat ass of yours you walk around shaking at the Honey Dipper, and the FBI is going to come for it," he said, smiling, knowing he had her. Tommy was from the streets, he knew how to speak her language.

"No they won't; I already cooperated," she snapped.

"Shut up, you think you know so much, Daisy Mae, what kind of name is Daisy Mae anyway? The fucking FBI is here, Daisy, and guess what, kiddo, you're going to jail, and not only are you going to prison, you won't have that money you're holding on to. And I know what you're thinking, you're thinking that you got, what, close to fifty thousand dollars and you can keep yourself safe." He smiled, having her all figured out.

"That's bullshit, that's my money."

"Not if I say so. I'm the law, I am the law! And you are going to cooperate with the state now and sign that affidavit or so help me God, I'm going downstairs and I'm going to let Agent Lang hang you. Don't believe me? Look here out the window," said Tommy, pointing to his little covert operation that he orchestrated along with his girlfriend, Vivian.

"You cooperate, not only will you get to keep your money, girlie, but you'll have the state to protect you from these assholes," said Tommy, hoping that she'd hurry up and sign the affidavit so he could go home, a job well done.

"I'm scared," said Daisy as she began to break down and cry at her reality, her life seemingly crashing.

"Don't be. It's gonna be all right. I won't let anything happen to you. I promise, Daisy, when I'm done you're gonna have a good life, trust me, a great, wonderful life, you hear me, kiddo?" he asked.

Little did she know that he would turn out to be one hundred on that. Daisy got off the stand and was escorted into the back of a room outside the courthouse doors where her cousin, Kimmie Sue, and her friend Billy Bob were waiting to say good-bye. It was decreed that she not have any contact with friends or family for her own protection. So she had no choice but to leave them behind, at least for now.

Finally, it was time to say good-bye to Tommy and his partner, Merva. Daisy didn't really care for her and it was apparent that Merva didn't care for her, either. But Tommy was Daisy's knight in shining armor. He was the one who, for some strange reason, did care. He wanted Daisy to make it. He wanted her to be all right. She hugged them both, but Tommy a little tighter.

"Call me when you get to Arizona and get settled. Don't worry, you have a security detail. You're better than safe and nothings gonna happen to you. All right?"

Daisy shook her head and kissed Tommy's cheek good-bye. Tommy and Merva watched her get into the vehicle before being driven away.

Daisy wanted to turn around, but didn't. There was no more looking back for her. The only thing she wanted to do was look forward.

Beverly Guess walked down Thirteenth Street, crossing the circle, making her way to the subway where she could catch the Broad Street line that would take her to North Philly, her stop Susquehanna and Dauphin. She emerged from the underground staircase and crossed the street to the bus stop. The number 39 would take her up to Twenty-third Street from Broad. She looked around at the busy street corner. Young mothers were walking by pushing their babies in strollers, Georgie Woods was outside, gathered around him a crowd of older men, laughing, joking, and waiting for their line in Don's Doo Barbershop. Beverly made it a point to stop and pay her respects to Mr. Woods, as did every single living, breathing soul that had the pleasure of his presence. Sitting on stoop after stoop were the older folks, sharing stories, laughter, and here and there a bottle of Mad Dog 20/20. A young hustler from the other side of the street approached her, flashing a two-by-three manila envelope filled with marijuana, folded in half and sealed.

"I got that gold, sis. Shit is crazy, I know you been looking for it."

"No, I haven't," she said to the young kid. *How do you know what I'm looking for?*

"No problem, I got that, though," he said, pushing the tiny manila envelope back into his jacket pocket.

Daisy kept making her way down the busy street. She thought of everything that had happened in the courthouse today. Daisy Mae Fothergill, when she told the jury that Nard was not with her on the night in question, had been as emotionless as a statue. Beverly never made eye contact with the girl. And the girl never looked in her direction. She just seemed to sit still, staring off into the distance looking at thin air as she offered her testimony to the prosecutor and the jury.

He ain't coming home, he ain't getting off. What was he thinking in the first place to get himself in all this trouble? It was all Beverly could think of, her son. The entire journey home was spent replaying everything that had transpired in that courtroom, as if there were a VCR in her brain. She couldn't believe that her baby boy had been charged with murder, and to think that he was actually capable of it was something she couldn't imagine.

In a way, Beverly blamed herself. She kept telling herself that maybe had she done this different or done that different none of this would have happened. She looked down Susquehanna Avenue. *I might as well walk myself on home.* The neighborhood was beginning to change. The movement of black power and fighting for power had slowly diminished in the seventies, and the eighties had brought with it a new era, and by the mid-eighties there was a new drug, called crack. Everyone agreed it was one of the most powerful drugs to hit the street. The righteous warned that it would wipe out the black man. No one paid the righteous any mind, but the righteous were right.

"It ain't nothing but cooked-up cocaine," one guy argued.

"Man, it's cooked up all right, with everything cooked in it from rat poison to ammonia. That ain't no real cocaine they selling in those vials, that shit'll kill you. Didn't you hear about them people bought some of that crack and was falling out and needing to be resuscitated?" responded another. Beverly had heard a hundred and one stories about this new powerful drug. However, she didn't really pay the stories any mind. She had heard of people purifying and freebasing cocaine. She even had a few friends that she knew every now and then indulged, but she figured whatever people were doing in the privacy of their own homes was their business. How in the world would it ever affect her and her life when she didn't do drugs?

The bus went by her just as she reached the corner of her block. *I can walk myself faster than you can carry me, Mr. Bus Man.* The smell of pork fried rice and fried chicken was coming from Wu's Chinese and American Cuisine and the stench in the air hit her nose as she turned the corner. Beverly looked at several young black men loitering outside Wu's takeout spot playing craps against the wall as they stayed on the lookout for the police. They had already been warned one hundred and ninety-nine times about shooting dice, gambling, and loitering on the corner.

"How's Nard, Ms. Beverly?" asked Chuck, one of the youngsters shooting dice on the corner.

"He's making it," she said with a smile, walking by as the boys continued shooting craps.

"Hey, Mr. Clarence," she said as she walked by the Wilsons' porch. Mr. Clarence was walking up the steps to his front door.

"Well, hello, Beverly, how's Ray coming along? I heard his foot was acting up. Ms. Doris was telling us he had to go to the hospital last Sunday at church."

"Yeah, it was his gout flaring up again, but he's getting around pretty good now. I'ma tell him you asked for him," said Beverly.

"Yeah, you do that, tell him I said I'm still waiting to settle the score on that checkers match," said Mr. Clarence, smiling, as he closed his front door.

Beverly made it a few doors down, picked up some loose-leaf trash that was lying on the sidewalk, and then evened out two potted planters at the foot of the steps leading to her porch.

"What's going on, Beverly?" a familiar voice asked. She turned to see who was calling her name.

"Rev? What you doing on my block?" asked Beverly, extending her arms to hug an old friend.

"Well, you know, a brother gots to do what a brother gots to do," he said, looking around as if he were waiting for someone.

"Yeah, but you still ain't answer my question, Rev. What brings you on this side of town?" questioned Beverly, looking around trying to figure out what he was looking for.

"Well, it's like this..."

"That's right, let her know who you here for," ordered a voice from behind him.

"Damn, woman, scared me half to death," jumped Rev as he turned around.

"Oh, hi, Maeleen," said Beverly, looking at the thirty-something-year-old standing before her. *I don't know who she thinks she is, but Lord please tell me Rev ain't messing around with her.*

"Don't hi Maeleen me! It ain't none of your business what he's doing over here. He don't answer to you. He answers to me," said an angry Maeleen, shaking her finger in Beverly's face.

"I know you better get your finger out my face before I..."

"Before what? Be careful what you wish for, Beverly," said Maeleen, ready to go toe to toe about her man.

"You know what?" asked Beverly, confused, and trying to figure out what was going on. She had this half man half fool standing in front of her, and an angry black woman wanting something to fight about.

"What?" asked Maeleen, ready to jump all over Beverly's ass if she said something slick out her mouth.

"You ain't even worth it. Yo, Rev, you better get her," said Beverly, ready to jump Maeleen right back.

"Come on, baby, come on, that's my peoples right there, come on. You can't be coming outside acting all crazy like you ain't got no sense. I know this thing good, baby, but you gots to act right. Come on, let's go calm down," said Rev, attempting to quell a cat fight before it started.

"You better get her and take her on somewhere," yelled Beverly, as her Uncle Ray Ray came to the door.

"Everything all right out here?" he asked, opening the door as the theme to *The Rockford Files* could be heard playing in the background.

"No, it ain't all right. That crazy woman from across the street," said Beverly, pointing to Maeleen leading Rev across the street.

"And don't let me catch you messing with my man again," hollered Maeleen for the entire block to hear.

"She's crazy, Uncle Ray Ray. All I was doing was standing outside talking to Donna's brother, Rev."

"Listen, I been done told you about them peoples over there. Her and her God damn mammee. Both them crows be out there digging up dirt and shit off dead people's graves. They're witches, her momma is a damn voodoo doctor, and she can put some roots on you like ain't nobody's business. I'm telling you what I know. That crazy bat been done set our house on fire without lighting a match."

"Uncle, I swear, you should have seen Rev, he seen her coming and he couldn't even open his mouth, couldn't even talk, and that's all Rev does is run his mouth. I can't believe he didn't say nothing. He just stood there and let her talk to me like that."

"That's how they do 'em. Trust me, if she gets a hold of him real good, he won't never talk to none of y'all no more without Maeleen telling him what to say," said Ray Ray, already knowing the 411 on his witch-brewing neighbors from across the street. "I watched that girl's mammee and she was a voodoo witch doctor. She stayed digging dirt out there in Mt. Vernon Cemetery right there off Thirty-third and Lehigh. I'm telling you what I know. And if Revere knows what's good for him, he'd get the hell away from her."

"I better tell Donna," said Beverly, picking up the phone to call her best friend.

"You better tell Donna, but hell, Donna can't save his black ass from no Maeleen. She got him and it's probably too late."

"Uncle Ray Ray, what you talking about it's probably too late."

"What I said, once them people get a hold on you, can't nobody save you. Donna and the rest of them can kiss Rev goodbye," said Uncle Ray Ray, slowly limping on his bad foot back to his favorite lounging chair. "How'd that boy make out today?" he said, asking about Nard.

"Well, it don't look good. Some stripper girl claimed she was paid to say Nard was with her and when she took the stand, she said he really wasn't," said Beverly, wishing there was something she could do to help her son.

"Nope, that don't sound good at all," said Uncle Ray Ray, already knowing Nard's fate. "That boy could have been somebody. Nard started selling them drugs and running them streets and they got a hold of him, and once the streets get you, they don't let you go." He mumbled something else, then tuned out his niece and tuned in to a *Sanford and Son* rerun.

"*Hill Street Blues* come on at nine o'clock," he added, as if Beverly needed to know the television lineup.

Beverly picked up the phone hanging on the wall and called Donna, her best friend for the past twenty-five years. First thing Donna asked about was Nard. Beverly told her everything that had transpired in the courtroom and all the drama that unfolded.

"It don't look good for him. I just don't know what to do," said Beverly, beginning to feel the stress of the past six months since Nard had been arrested and held without bail.

"Don't worry, I'll be right up in there with you tomorrow. Damn, I wish I could have been there today," Donna added, just before Beverly remembered why she had really called her in the first place.

"Wait, guess who I just seen?"

"Who?"

"That damn Rev."

"My brother, Rev?"

"Yeah, honey, with my neighbor Maeleen."

"Oh, snap, hold up, Bev, don't you know it's a mess, honey, Revere done brought that Maybeline girl over here and Momma told him she didn't like her, not one bit. Don't you know he got mad and ain't spoke to nobody since."

"Aww, Rev know he not right, he better talk to his momma, that's the only momma he got."

"Momma said let him go on with Maybeline..."

"Maeleen?" interrupted Beverly, trying to help her friend get the woman's name right.

"Maeleen, Maybeline, shit is all the same, Beverly. Don't nobody care what that woman's name is. Momma told Revere don't come back in her house with her no more."

"Well, you know, Uncle Ray Ray said she's a witch, her and her momma is both witches, and she's into that root shit or whatever the hell it is."

"I believe it 'cause she came in here and sat down on the sofa and I don't know what the hell kind of smell she got in her ass but you can still smell her in the air. It's a funny smell, too, the weirdest thing."

"What do you mean?" asked Beverly.

"Bev, I swear to God if you come over here right now and sit down on the sofa where she was sitting you can smell her, and she was here like two weeks ago and ain't been back."

"Did you try to wipe the sofa down or something?"

"Girl, Momma done tried everything, even ammonia. But the weird thing is, you only smell her if you sit directly behind her. If you sit at the other end of the sofa you don't smell a thing."

"And it hasn't worn off?"

"Nope, I don't know what to say, but this bitch ass is permanently in my momma's sofa. I know that."

"What in the world is wrong with Revere?"

"Who the hell knows, all my brothers is retards. I don't understand it. They always get hooked up with crazy ass women and end up putting everybody out their minds. Revere is doing too good for himself to be messing with the wrong woman."

"Well, you know she got like four or five kids?"

"Four or five kids? He don't even like kids. He won't help me with none of my foster kids. I asked him to watch Trey and Lashawn so I could go to the store and he acted like he was gonna die. I know he done lost his mind now. Rev don't mess with no women with no kids, ever!"

"Yeah, they're something awful, too. Them kids of hers is real bad. I swear I ain't never lie."

"You know what, let me call you back. I'ma tell my momma and see what she says about all this."

"Okay, I'll be here, just call me if you need me. Oh, wait, you gonna meet me in the morning at the welfare office?"

"Yeah, girl, I need them food stamps, too. You know Hong's be cashing them shits in, girl, seven dollars for every ten."

"No way, Wu's only gives me six."

"Fuck Wu's, you better cash them chumpies in with Hong's, honey, seven dollars is good money all day."

"It sure is. I'll see you in the morning and then we'll go to court."

Beverly hung up the phone. She couldn't help but to think about her son and all he must be going through. She remembered his outburst and the way she had looked at him. Their eyes had locked for a split second, and she saw right through him without him saying a word. She could see his fear, she could see his anger and she could see his pain. *There's got to be something that the lawyer can do to save his life. The girl done said he wasn't with her. What is going to happen to him now? What's going to happen to my son?*

SILENCE IS GOLDEN

Liddles was parked in the back of Pathmark's Shopping Center at Forty-fifth and Sansom Street out in West Philadelphia. His man, Luck, pulled into the lot driving a red Volvo with a black rag top. Luck got out of the car, his short frame moving quickly as he hopped into Liddles's yellow Volvo, graced with the same custom black rag.

"You good?" asked Luck, greeting his man with a shake of the hand as he closed the car door.

"Yeah, you got that?" asked Liddles as Luck passed him a plastic City Blue clothing bag.

"You said for the .45, right?" asked Luck.

"Yeah, or the .38," said Liddles as he looked in the bag, making sure Luck came correct. "This is it," Liddles said, shaking his head as he looked at the silencer.

"You straight?" Luck asked slapping a five before hopping out of the car.

"I'm good and plenty," joked Liddles. He watched Luck get back into his Volvo before pulling out of the grocery store lot.

"I needed this," he said out loud to himself, thankful for

Luck, as his cell phone rang. His man Reese had the plate information, including name, address, date of birth, and social security number.

Truth be told, Liddles would fall in line to run the city. It was his destiny. His brother Poncho never wanted Liddles around, he always kept him on the sideline, always kept him out of harm's way, but it was destined for him to run the city.

"I don't want you out here and that's that. Go home!" He could hear his brother Poncho screaming at him to get off the block.

"How you gonna tell me I'm not to be out here and you're out here. Nobody's gonna have your back like me. I'm supposed to be out here with you."

"Why?" shouted Poncho, tired of arguing with his kid brother. "Why the fuck you think you supposed to be out here? You not my keeper!"

"Yes I am, I am my brother's keeper," said Liddles, knowing the infamous line from the scriptures about Cain and Abel.

"Nigga, no you not, I'm your keeper. Get your young ass in the house, you understand? And you do what I tell you to. If I need you, I know where you at, but you not my keeper, you understand?" He could remember his brother telling him, "Go on, man, go in the house where you'll be safe. This shit is a jungle out here. I don't want to have to worry about you, too."

See, I should have been there, like I told you, now you know I would have saved you.

It didn't matter, though, because now that Poncho was gone, Liddles was where he wanted to be, and he had taken Poncho's place. He filled the void that Poncho left behind. Who better to fill his brother's shoes? And they fit perfectly.

The only thing missing in his life was his brother, and for his brother, he would kill everything moving, it was only a matter of time.

"My case is going down the drain. They're going to hang this guy, literally," Bobby DeSimone casually explained. "I told him before this trial even started to take the plea. I told him that the police had found the girl and he didn't listen. Had he listened to me, we wouldn't be in this mess," said Bobby as he stuffed a piece of salmon in his mouth. "Are these the best mashed potatoes in the world or what?"

"They are," agreed Joanne.

"So, anyway, this fuck bag DA is sitting there smirking at me the whole time. I just wanted to put his head in a chokehold and pull out his eyelashes with a pair of tweezers. And this girl, this Daisy Mae Fothergill bitch, just completely sank the entire case with her fucking testimony. 'No, I never saw him before in my life.' Thanks a lot, Daisy, and then this fucking make pretend cop, Delgado, takes the girl and calmly and quietly escorts this stripper slut whore away into seclusion in some comfy witness protection program."

"Really?" asked Joanne, listening to how serious the case was.

"Really, she's probably in fucking Disney World stripping for Mickey, Donald, and Pluto as we speak."

"Wow, I love Disney World," commented Joanne, in utter ignorance and agreement at the same time.

"I'm serious, Jo, I'm fucking serious over here."

"Honey, so am I. You know I love the castle."

Bobby wondered if she even got half the conversations he had with her. He looked at her breasts and thought about what her only contribution to his life was. His mind pictured himself fondling her naked body with her legs spread wide apart. *Stay focused, remember the kid, remember the case, I have to stay focused.*

"You know, you are really stressed. I can fix that," she said in a devious whisper. She realized he wasn't paying attention to what she was saying. "Hey, Bobby, you are so not listening to me," she said, nudging his arm.

"What?" he asked, upset she interrupted his moment.

"I can't believe you, you weren't listening to a word I was saying."

"Umm," he said as he played her back. "You said, 'I can fix that.'" He smiled; he was right.

She smiled back, and it was as if those four words were all she needed to hear; they made her night. For Joanne it meant he was paying attention to her, even if she didn't think he was.

"Come on. You done, let's get out of here?"

"Sure," she agreed.

She watched Bobby rise up from the table and take out enough money from his pocket to cover the bill and a hefty tip. He never asked for the bill, just left the money, already knowing how much it would be, that was how often they had dinner at Cutters.

Just as the elevator doors closed, Bobby pressed P2. They reached the lower garage level where Bobby had parked his car. His mind was scrambling as he thought of losing everything. The case was too big and was receiving too much media coverage for him to come out looking like the biggest loser ever. He had everything riding on this one. If he won, the key to the city would be his. He'd be noted as one of the best criminal attorneys in the city. He needed the win, just like Nard needed an alibi. But Nard didn't have an alibi and it didn't look like DeSimone would be a winner.

He opened the door and got into the car. He put the key in the ignition and turned the engine on. He sat there thinking of what his next move could be, his next witness, his next line of questioning, and truth was, at the moment, he didn't have a clue what he was going to do. The girl, Daisy, and her testimony had his case sunk in the mud.

"Hello, Bobby, don't you hear me knocking on the window," said Jo, her face to the window as she looked at him, wondering why he wouldn't unlock the door for her.

She tapped on the glass again and he looked at her. She was bent down with her face pressed up against the glass staring him dead in the eyes.

"Are you kidding me? Open the fucking door, Bobby! Why are you looking at me like that?"

His mind was reeling with thoughts of frustration, anxiety, and impatience for the answers he so desperately needed, and just as he lifted his finger, pressed the button, and unlocked the door for her to get inside, inspiration struck and he had the most amazing revelation.

"What in the hell, Bobby, I'm standing out there tapping on the window and you're like a zombie," she said when she finally was seated next to him.

"Wait!" he said, scaring her half to death. "Wait one minute!" he yelled. "They came through the window! Jo, that's it, they came through the window!"

"Yeah, who?" she asked, as if he was nuts.

"They came through the window and grabbed the guy. That was his original statement, that's the first thing Nard said to me," said Bobby, his head ready to explode from the rush of anxiety and overwhelming excitement. He was sweating.

"Who?"

"The bad guys. That's it, that's it, that's the key, the window," he said, loudly enough to echo throughout the parking lot. "Suck my dick, Zone!" he shouted, looking like a madman.

"Who's Zone?" she wanted to know, hoping it wasn't competition for her.

"Yes, the window, I have to go," he said, realizing he needed to get back to his office. He had tremendous tenacity and an excellent work ethic. He would fit all his pieces together, as if he were playing Battleship, and tomorrow, he would blow Zone right out of the water.

"You have to go? Go where?" asked Jo, not wanting to give up date night.

"Back to the office; I can't believe it. Fucking around with this stripper bitch, I'm all throwed off and I'm losing, but the window is open, baby!" he screamed at the top of his lungs, his mind now moving a mile a minute. "I'm sorry, here, I got to go," he said, reaching in his pocket and pulling out cab fare.

"You're not taking me home?" she asked, as he handed her the money, reached over her, and opened the car door, pushing it wide for her to exit.

"No, I can't, I have work to do. I have to go. No, you have to go. Out... the door," he confidently said, as if she were an afterthought.

"But, I thought..."

"Jo, no thinking for you, it's not the time, you have to get going and call me and let me know you're home," he said, helping scoot her ass out of the passenger seat, pushing her butt and slapping her ass. Then he used his hand to usher her to close the door. Pulled off and left her standing there as his red taillights lit up the parking lot. He reached the exit, pulled out into the street, and turned into the oncoming traffic.

He's so unbelievable, she said as she counted the money he had left her with. *One hundred and seventy-six dollars? Why would he give me all this money to take a cab?* She decided to take the bus, using her monthly bus pass, as she did to get back and forth to work, and tomorrow she'd give him back his money.

The ringing of the phone not only startled Tommy and Vivian but woke their black Lab, Prince, who started barking and howling as if he were staring up at a full moon. Tommy rolled over and answered the phone as Vivian looked at the clock.

"Prince, shut up!" they yelled at the dog simultaneously.

"It's three in the morning, Tommy. Who is it?"

"Okay, I'm on my way," said Tommy, hanging up the phone.

"What now."

"It looks like a young woman was raped and killed a few hours ago," he lied. "Even on my time off, I gotta work. They gave the case to me. I got to go," said Tommy, as he threw back the covers, got up, and walked down the hall to the bathroom.

Vivian was going to share her big secret with him over breakfast, but the timing once again was off for her.

"I swear, if I could just get one good night's sleep. If it's not you, it's me. If it's not me, it's my mother. If it's not my mother, it's your mother. I need a vacation."

"Me, too, Viv, me, too," said Tommy, kissing his girlfriend before he slipped on his clothes.

"You're not going to take a shower?" she asked, as if he needed one.

"No, I don't have time."

"You're wearing the same clothes you had on yesterday?"

"Viv, I don't have time."

"Aren't you scheduled to testify in court today on that Somerset case?"

"Fuck! You're right," he said, doubling back and opening his closet door. He pulled a red tie off a hanger, then a green one. "Hey Viv, which one do you think?" he asked holding up the ties.

"Go with the green, it really makes that shirt from yesterday pop, honey."

"Don't be a wise-ass."

"Just kiss me good-bye," she said as he bent over the bed, hugging her and pecking her lips. "God, Tommy, you didn't even brush your teeth."

"I'm going to work. I'm not going to see my mother, Viv," he said, walking down the hallway.

"Geez, maybe we should go visit your mother so you'll take a bath and brush your teeth, for God's sake."

"You hate my mother," he hollered, closing the door behind him.

"You're right, don't bathe, don't brush, the hell with it," Vivian mumbled to herself before turning off the night light next to her bed and wrapping herself back up in her covers.

Tommy started his engine. He looked at his watch. It was three-thirty-six in the morning. *What the fuck is wrong with Patricio, calling my house at three in the morning? What if Vivian had answered the phone? This better be good, it better be a fucking emergency.* Tommy checked his rearview mirror to see if he was being tailed. He already knew the possibilities were endless.

He traveled down Broad Street, passing the Spectrum, where the 76ers played. He turned right into the Naval Yard and followed the signs for the Naval Hospital. The meeting place was always the same.

Tommy parked his car and walked into the hospital, following the signs for the emergency room. He patiently picked up a magazine and took a seat in the waiting area. Within three minutes, Patricio Gambiani, whom everyone called Patty for short, took a seat next to him.

"What the fuck is wrong with you, calling my house in the middle of the night, Patricio?"

"Calm down, I used a pay phone," said Patricio.

"So what's so urgent you had to get me up in the middle of the night?"

"You're being investigated by Internal Affairs."

"For what? I've done nothing. Why would they be investigating me?" he hissed at his cousin, wishing his family would keep him out of their business. He never allowed himself to engage in or be around criminal activity, and for the most part kept himself clean despite the persistent opportunities to be dirty. He knew his family. All his life, he was kept from them, because of his father and his father's father. After his mother and his father separated and decided to get divorced, it got really ugly. So she was scared, and all Tommy remembered was moving around a lot. His mother was Sicilian, real olive complexion, with dark features, just like him. He was lucky; they moved to the Dominican Republic, and with the bright sun and a few months of learning the language, they soon blended right in. His mother changed their last names to Delgado, and Charlie Gatto never found her. It was Tommy and Sammy who found their father, as young men years later after their mother died. Once reunited with their father, they decided to stay in the States, and Tommy joined the force and Sammy joined his father's organization.

"I don't know, but let's see...how about your past and present drug abuse, our family's affiliation with organized crime...um...your brother just robbed another bank yesterday afternoon and got away with two million dollars."

"Sammy?"

"You have any other brothers someone failed to inform me

of?" asked Patricio. He couldn't help being a wise-ass. He was simply bringing his cousin up to speed on current family affairs. He picked up a newspaper, covered his face, and continued to whisper through the pages.

That was the straw that broke the camel's back. *What the fuck? Sammy hit another one and got away?* Tommy questioned to himself, a smile spreading across his face.

"Are you sure?" he asked, as if Patricio didn't know what he was talking about.

"Listen, all I was told to tell you is that you're being investigated by Internal Affairs and to watch your back. And yes, your brother's celebrating in Las Vegas as we speak." Patricio smiled. He smacked his cousin's leg, squeezing it gently before he got up to leave.

Tommy sat silently, still trying to think of who in the department could possibly be investigating him. He had thought he had the department fooled for such a long time. *They're probably right under my nose and I don't even know it.* He didn't have the slightest clue, but his family would find out, because the same way the state had moles, well, so did Tommy's family.

KNOCK KNOCK

Day Two

Beverly heard the banging at the door. Tired, she rolled over and pulled the covers over her head. She heard her Uncle Ray Ray's footsteps down the hall.

"What's wrong with people, banging on people's doors and waking people up out their sleep?" asked Uncle Ray Ray as he walked by Beverly's bedroom door.

"You got it, Uncle Ray Ray?"

"I guess I might as well," he responded. She heard the staircase floorboards creek with each step he took as he made his way down the stairs.

He peeked out of the peephole and saw his son, Chris, standing at the door, shifting from side to side.

"That you, Chris?" he asked, wondering whether his eyes were deceiving him.

"Yeah, it's me, Dad."

Ray Ray opened the door and faced his son, happy to see him, until he got a good look. "What in the world is wrong with you? You sick? You look terrible."

"Pop, I need your help. My car broke down and I can't get to work."

"You was on your way to work looking like that?" Ray Ray asked, staring his son in the face. He held the door for him, letting him pass.

Chris, unable to look his father in the eyes, continued to shift and move aimlessly. His lips were chapped, and he smelled of stale burned sulfur.

"You smell funny," commented Ray Ray.

"It's just from sweating trying to fix my car."

"And your eyes look funny, like they're about to pop out your head. You sure you're okay, son?"

"Yeah, Pop, I'm fine, really. I just need some money to my get car rolling, you know, so I can get to work. I'm already late and I don't want to get in trouble," he said hastily, as if time was of the essence.

Beverly had made her way downstairs and peeped around the corner of the kitchen wall. She was being nosy and was eavesdropping on her cousin and her uncle, but for good reason.

Look at him, he looks like he's about to pounce all over Uncle Ray Ray if Uncle Ray Ray doesn't give him some money. I wonder what's wrong with him? This was the first time Beverly had ever seen someone high on crack cocaine, but it would be far from the last.

"I got to go upstairs, unless I got some money in my jacket pocket. Hold on, let me see what I got," said Uncle Ray Ray, retreating to the closet by the front door to check his jacket. Beverly walked around the corner and entered the kitchen.

"Hey, Chris, how's life treating you?"

"Man, you scared me half to death," he said nervously, turning around to face his cousin.

Just then there was another knock at the door.

"Who in the world could this be?" said Beverly as she walked to the front door and looked out the peephole. "It's too early in the morning," she noted.

Crystal. What in the world is she doing here? Beverly opened the door. Standing in the cold morning air was Nard's girlfriend, the mother of his nine-month-old daughter, Dayanna.

"Crystal, come on in here, child, and get that baby out the cold," said Beverly, like any concerned grandmother. "What are you doing out this early in the morning?" she asked, figuring the girl wanted to go to court with her.

"My mother put me out," said Crystal, lowering her head and pretending to be fixing the baby's hat. "She said she told me not to bring no babies in her house and I can't go to school and she's real mad about that 'cause I don't have nobody to watch the baby and my mom has to work. She said she can't sleep with the baby crying and she needs her rest for work. She said I need to come here and live with you so Nard can help take care of the baby, since don't nobody here have a job to go to," said Crystal as Beverly sat back. She already knew where Crystal's mother was going.

"Well, you know I'm not gonna see my grandbaby out in the street. You and the baby might as well stay in Nard's room until your momma lets you come back home. I'm sure she'll get to missing you sooner or later and we can always work out some arrangements for me to keep Dayanna while you're at school."

"I don't know, I don't think I want to go back home, Ms. Beverly," said Crystal, happy she could stay with her boyfriend's mother.

"Umm, you gonna have to go home sooner or later, but as long as you go to school, I'll let you stay, but you going to school, you hear me? A young girl always needs her mother, and your mother I'm sure is missing you already, but you need to be in school," said Beverly, walking down the hall, Crystal right behind her.

"I will be, don't worry."

"And when you done at school, you come on in here and get your schoolwork done and take care of Dayanna, you understand? I'll help you, but you got to help yourself."

"Thanks, Dad," said Chris, hurrying as if he was about to sprint like a track runner.

"Okay, see you later, Beverly," he said, brushing past her quickly. He waved good-bye, closing the door behind him.

"Uncle Ray Ray, is it my imagination or did Chris just haul his ass out of here like the police was chasing him?"

"He's on something, did you see him? I don't know who the hell I just gave my money to, but that wasn't my son," said Uncle Ray Ray, worried for Chris, his only son. "He's grown, though, what can I do?"

"Hi, Uncle Ray Ray," said Crystal, all smiles.

"We got some new house guests," said Beverly. "Her momma done put her and the baby out, so I told her she can stay here with us for awhile until her momma lets her come back home."

"Oh, well, I see now, and what about the baby?" asked Uncle Ray Ray, not wanting to be bothered with no babies, even kin.

"I'm sure it won't be too long," said Beverly, kissing her granddaughter.

"I hope not, 'cause something tells me we're fittin' not to get no sleep up in here no time soon with a baby in the house," Uncle Ray Ray mumbled to himself as he made his way up the steps to his room. "I ain't got no money, a spook done came in here and took my little bit of pocket change. Now I got to get out here and try to get to one of those MAC machines," he mumbled some more.

Beverly watched as Ray Ray made his way up the staircase. "I got to get dressed and get down to the welfare office. And then me and my girlfriend, Donna, is going straight to the courthouse."

"Will Nard be there, will I get to see him?" asked Crystal, full of wonder and surprise.

Beverly couldn't help but to stop and think of her yesteryears when she was young and believed in love. "Yes, he'll be there at the courthouse." She smiled.

"Well, you think me and Dayanna can go with you?"

"Why not?" Beverly responded as she walked down the hall and up the stairs to get dressed. "Be ready in a half hour."

Vivian Lang arrived fifteen minutes late to work. Before she could even take off her coat, there was a knock at her door, The deputy in charge, Marshall Stevens, opened the door and peeked inside her office without waiting for a "who is it" or "come in."

"Deputy Stevens, how are you this morning?"

"Well, I'd be better, but criminals are making my life challenging," he said as he walked into her office. "I have two cases I'd like to send your way. The first is this abandoned baby case—mind you we got no leads. So far we've got seven babies that have been abandoned on the steps of the St. Agnes Mary Catholic Church in West Philadelphia in the last month. The church had installed video cameras after the fourth baby had been abandoned. However, the cameras aren't picking up anything for us to go on. You look at it, tell me if anything catches your eye. We think it's a religious cult, some form of worship, possible sacrifice."

"You mean leaving babies out on church steps to freeze to death."

"Yeah, exactly." He paused for a second, then quickly moved on. "And the other case, well, you're gonna love this. We had another bank robbery yesterday. From the looks of the video surveillance, which you are really gonna love, it looks like the same guys, but again, there's nothing to fall back on from the tapes. These guys got away in the middle of the afternoon, in broad daylight, and we have nothing to go on. See if you see anything; I need a fresh pair of eyes." He placed two video surveillance tapes from the bank and from the church on her desk.

"Well, I suggest we get some work done around here and make some arrests. Hell, I hate having to take down the innocent and law-abiding, so just remember that it's much better if we arrest the people who actually committed the crime. That's the way, uh-huh, uh-huh, I like it," he said, not singing the song at all.

"I'll look at these tapes right away, sir."

"You do that, Lang, and let me know what your findings are by noon."

"I'm on it, sir."

Vivian Lang watched as Deputy Stevens closed her office door behind him. She picked up her phone and paged her assistant, Sharon, who had a cup of coffee, extra cream, extra sugar, just the way Vivian liked it, on her desk in nine point seven seconds.

"Can you get a Danish from the machine?" asked Vivian as she handed her money to Sharon, not waiting for an answer. She dimmed the lights, closed her window blinds, and began to watch the videotape recordings of crime. She took another sip of her coffee. Feeling woozy, she sat down, her stomach churning and boiling inside her like a volcano about to erupt. She grabbed the trashcan from under her desk just in the nick of time and puked her strawberry cheese Danish and cup of morning Joe into the trashcan. Her hands felt clammy, her body felt faint, and if it hadn't been for Deputy Stevens's personal appearance this morning she'd be turning around and heading home.

What in the world is wrong with me?

She had buzzed for Sharon, her assistant, who was standing in the doorway watching her vomit into her trashcan.

"Oh, my God, are you okay? I have some tissues. Here you go," she said, placing them near Vivian but not wanting to get too close. "And let me get you some cold water from the fountain," said Sharon, quickly leaving the room as Vivian vomited another round of last night's dinner into the trashcan before returning in less than seven point two seconds with the water from the water fountain. "Are you okay, ma'am? Maybe you're pregnant, wouldn't that be great? I just love babies. Should I get someone to help you?"

"No, no, Sharon. I'm fine…I'll be fine. I'm not pregnant, thank you very much, you can go back to your desk. Everything's fine, trust me," said Vivian, waving her too-excited, too-over-the-top, happy, so happy secretary away from her with her happy, so happy ideas of pregnancy. Vivian looked at her, began to vomit again, and at the same time shooed the girl out the door with her hand.

"Close my door, please," ordered Vivian between gasps of air as she upchucked one more time into the trashcan. She watched Sharon close the door behind her.

Maybe I'm pregnant. The thought was ludicrous. *Maybe I have stomach cancer.* The possibility was scary. She had no idea what was wrong with her, but she used the tissue Sharon had brought her, wiped her mouth, picked up her phone, and made an emergency appointment for later on in the day. She lay down on her sofa, looked at the tapes, and cleared them, finding nothing on them that could help either case.

Tommy Delgado sat patiently next to his partner, Merva Ross, in the courtroom waiting to give testimony should they be called. They had been the crime scene detectives on the Somerset murder case and were both assigned to it. It was Tommy and Merva who had arrested Nard and taken him into custody, where he was held without bail and transferred to CFCF for the last six months. It was Tommy and Merva who had convinced Daisy to turn state and not give Nard the alibi he so desperately needed. Over the past year, they had accomplished a lot working as partners.

The courtroom was packed, with familiar and unfamiliar faces alike scattered across the room. The prosecutor had wrapped up his case in one day. Cut and dried, no questions asked. Zone put Daisy Mae Fothergill on the stand, and she failed to give the defendant, Nard, an alibi, blowing a hole in the defense's case, and after that was done, Zone called it a day. The state felt it had enough circumstantial evidence to try and convict Bernard Guess of the murders of Jeremy Tyler and Lance Robertson. The deaths of Saunta Davis and DaShawn Davis still were marked open and unsolved. They had no leads, no witnesses, and no suspects. An open homicide file with no suspects remained simply that until evidence of some nature surfaced and detectives had something to go on.

Lucille Davis sat quietly in the back of the courtroom every day, clutching a tiny photo of her grandson, DaShawn. She knew what had happened, because DaShawn had told her. She knew something was terribly wrong when she and her daughter had heard the shots down the hall and her grandbaby was still outside. Saunta, her daughter, looked out the peephole for her son, DaShawn. It was then she saw Nard leaving the apartment and that's when she went to the living room window and began calling for her son outside. He had promised to go down the street to the corner store and come right back. Why couldn't he have done that and come right back? Instead, DaShawn watched the boy Quinny Day win the lucky pot in a crap game. Then, he came into the building as shots rang out.

"Hey, Nard, be careful, they shooting in the building," the little boy would tell an armed and dangerous Nard, who had actually been the one doing all the shooting. That split moment had sealed his fate and his mother's. And Lucille Davis knew exactly what happened to her grandson and her daughter. She knew everything.

"Boy, get in here. You had me sick," she said to DaShawn, hugging her son as he walked through the door calm, cool and collected.

"They were shooting down the hallway."

"I just saw Nard," said the boy.

"That's who that was coming out the doorway," said the girl, looking at her mother, "the boy Nard."

"Mmm-hmm, I bet everybody in that apartment is dead. We better call 911 and report the gunshots. That's all we can do. But don't tell nobody you seen nothing. You hear me?" she said, looking at her daughter and then her grandson.

"Yes, ma'am, I won't say anything," said the little boy, shaking his head, scared to death.

The next day, the police found the three dead bodies in the apartment down the hall. Then one week later, he came back to murder her daughter and her grandson, shooting them down like dogs in the hallway as they had almost reached the apartment door. She had been right there in the kitchen when she heard them in the hallway. She thought nothing of it, until she heard gunshots, her daughter's screams, and then silence. It was the eerie silence that came with death. As she looked out the peephole of her apartment door, she saw their blood-stained bodies, and him, standing over her daughter, before stuffing the gun in his pocket, turning away, and walking down the hallway. While she was looking out the peephole, she reached around the wall, her hand grasped the phone, and she dialed 911. Stepping back into the kitchen, she whispered that her daughter and grandson had been shot and needed an ambulance.

"Please, please come quick. Please send somebody for me, my baby's been shot. My baby's been shot," the fifty-three-year-old woman cried into the phone. It was a tragic loss, altering her perception and existence. For her, after the loss of her only daughter and only grandson, nothing would be the same again in life, ever. And while she knew what happened and could have said something to the police, she was afraid for her life, and she refused to speak to the police and never ever would.

Euretha Giles sat in the fourth row of the courtroom every day in the same spot. She had three sons, one from a previous marriage and two from her murdered husband, Lester. Now, for Euretha, the death of Lester brought a lot of mixed emotions. Theirs was a tumultuous relationship, a roller-coaster ride that ended with them in separate bedrooms under the same roof. Did Euretha miss Lester? She missed his companionship. *I'll get a dog, thank you, don't worry about me.* Truth was, ol' Euretha knew more than Lester thought she knew. She knew he had made the ladies in the building have sex with him in exchange for rent. *He would say to me, "I'm going to collect the rent." You think I don't know what Mr. Man was collecting, 'cause where's the money, then?*

Where is it at? All and all, he raised his boys, provided decently, and never was abusive. What more could you say? *Nothing, that's it, nothing else to say for him.*

Euretha sat in the courtroom. She just had to be there. She knew whatever had happened to Lester had something to do with that Daisy Mae. All she remembered about that tragic day was a lot of banging on the front door like someone was desperate to get into the building.

"Lester, go see what all that damn banging is down there why don't you?"

"Why, what do you care for? Let them bang."

"See, don't blame me when you go downstairs and there's a hole in the damn wall. Then you'll be mad."

He picked up his sweater, threw it over his shoulders, and slipped on his slippers.

"Don't go messing with my fancy TV and remote control unit, leave it just like it is."

"I'm not sitting here watching no football all night, Lester. I want to watch my Lawrence Welk programming."

"Woman, has you lost your mind? I'm not fittin' to sit up in here looking at that old wrinkly white man on my brand-new thirty-two-inch Magnavox television set when my football game is on. The Cowboys is playing tonight," he said, laughing at her, knowing he was getting his way. "Listen, if you're lucky, you might get a commercial break, maybe a little five minutes or something extra, but I'm watching my game," said Lester, laughing at his wife as he walked out the door.

"Whatever, weasel," she mumbled to herself.

"Hey!" he shouted, "I heard that," he said.

She went over to Lester's chair and sat down in it. He had the best seat in the house. She grabbed the remote, changing the channel until she found the station she was looking for. She even turned up the volume a bit and sat back and relaxed, watching her programming. Poor Lester, had it not been for Lawrence Welk, Euretha might have heard the intruder and the attack on Lester downstairs in Daisy Mae's apartment. But she didn't.

She had watched as Daisy got down off the stand. *Yeah, honey, you got yourself in a whole world of trouble, Missy. I guess I won't be seeing you no more. I might as well go ahead and get that apartment unit of yours ready to rent again.*

Truth was Euretha didn't have to do much of anything. She had a two-hundred-thousand-dollar life insurance policy that had been in effect at the time of the brutal beating that led to Lester's death, which the police had ruled a homicide. And in a couple of weeks, when underwriting was done with their paper-pushing process, ol' Euretha would be sitting pretty on a fancy island, sipping one of those fruity-looking piña coladas and doing the limbo. *Don't forget about the rent.* Oh, yeah, and the rent, hope everybody had it on time 'cause there'd be no more bargaining. It was a new day, a new way, and you had to pay. *That's right, honey, make sure they know it's a new sheriff in this town and her name is Euretha Giles.*

Bobby DeSimone pushed open the double wooden doors that led into the courtroom. He had worked on the Somerset murder case all night long, gone through at least three pots of coffee. And now, he was ready. He had the perfect defense lined up. After yesterday, and the damaging testimony of Daisy Mae Fothergill, he had to make a comeback. This was it.

"Are we ready, Mr. DeSimone?" the judge bellowed from the stand.

"Yes, Your Honor, yes, we are," said DeSimone, standing straight and tall. "I'd like to call Bernard Guess to the stand, Your

Honor," said DeSimone, the entire courtroom buzzing with excitement. He felt it was the only way to save the kid's life. He had no choice but to put him on the stand. With only half an hour of prep time, he had told Nard that the only way to get out of this trap he was caught in was to tell the truth. And at the end of the day, the truth could easily set him free.

After Bernard was finished telling the story of how the two would-be gunmen came from down the hall holding his friend, Ponando "Poncho" Fernandez, in a choke hold with a gun to his head demanding drugs and money, he knew that if he didn't do something, he would have been murdered, too. By the time DeSimone had finished with Bernard Guess, he was merely a man who was protecting himself from would-be robbers, a man who was lucky to have escaped with his life. And the bottom line was, because they came through that back window with fully loaded weapons, Bernard Guess had every right to protect himself. It was a classic case of self-defense. Was it wrong to get the girl Daisy Mae Fothergill involved? Of course it was. DeSimone made sure that he and the jury knew that, because if that was all that the district attorney had, that simply wasn't going to be enough. When DeSimone asked Nard to explain why he had asked Daisy Mae Fothergill to lie in the first place, he solemnly told the jury that he was scared and didn't know what else to do. The truth was the kid was weeks shy of his twenty-first birthday and had never been arrested before, not even as a juvenile. He graduated high school, but went from basketball courts to hustling.

Of course, Barry Zone attempted to redirect, but Nard simply continued making himself out to be the victim just as DeSimone had coached him to.

After Zone concluded his line of questioning, DeSimone

brought Detective Tommy Delgado to the stand. Delgado unfortunately did nothing but offer testimony that backed up the self-defense theory by testifying that the would-be robbers, Jeremy Tyler and Lance Robertson, did in fact climb a tree and come through an open window in the bathroom of the third-floor row home. It was also Detective Delgado he requested to read aloud the criminal records of Jeremy Tyler and Lance Robertson, as both had served time in prison for aggravated assault, gun charges, and drugs.

After he had finished with Detective Delgado, he called to the stand a ballistics specialist, who confirmed that the gun found in Jeremy Tyler's hand was in fact the gun used to kill Ponando Fernandez, also known as Poncho. However, it was not the gun that was used to kill Lance Robertson. The crime lab specialists also confirmed that the gun used to kill Lance Robertson was the same gun that had been used to kill Jeremy Tyler. Thank God the gun had not been found. DeSimone could only imagine the possibilities, thinking of how his client had merely thrown it away in a trashcan.

Once he was done with his hired ballistics specialist, he moved on to forensics and the fibers found on the bathroom window at the scene, which offered substantial evidence that Nard was in fact defending himself from burglars.

Then DeSimone pulled out the big gun, one of his closest friends from law school, Bernie Madofften. Bernie had become a top-notch expert in the psychiatric study of serial killers. He was very famous, very notable, and trustworthy, and his opinions were regarded as definitive by his peers in the professions of psychology and psychiatry. And of course his testimony backed Nard's testimony, wherein Nard claimed he panicked, was afraid for his own life, and had a complete out-of-body experience and didn't mean to kill or harm the intruders.

By the time DeSimone was finished marking exhibits, questioning forensics and the police, and assisting Nard in his apparent and seemingly honest and truthful testimony, DeSimone had not only made Jeremy Tyler and Lance Robertson look like America's Most Wanted, but it was apparent that not only were they hardened criminals, they were completely responsible for their own deaths, brought on by their own actions, and technically deserved what they got when they climbed through the window that fateful night. He let his last witness go, put his fists on his hips, spread his legs apart, looking like a full grown Peter Pan, and told the judge, "I have no more witnesses, Your Honor."

The judge and DeSimone turned to Barry Zone, whose job was to put Nard in jail. "Will you be cross-examining, Mr. Zone?" he asked once again. And once again, Zone's answer was the same.

"No, Your Honor, not at this time."

DeSimone couldn't help but look over at Zone, intentionally mimicking the sly eye slant of a fox. *Gotcha!* He smiled, showed his pearly whites as Barry Zone held up his middle finger, pretended to smile back, then rolled his eyes.

Liddles, his trusty binoculars in hand, sat in his beat-up old navy blue van, just as he had yesterday and the day before, and watched as Wink and his family got into the silver Oldsmobile. Their faces were somber, and no one said a word. They didn't seem as happy and jubilant as they had been yesterday. His sister had already taken a cab home, after filling him on the day's courtroom drama. At least it was looking better for Nard, and Nard had finally gotten a chance to tell what happened that night.

He turned the key, started the car, and began following the

Tyler family. This time he didn't lose them, and Wink never noticed the van following him even as it pulled up in front of his mother's house.

Liddles watched the house carefully and waited as the family went inside. Wink emerged fifteen minutes later with a laundry bag in tow. *My brother for yours,* he thought to a dead Jeremy.

Timing would be crucial, but other than that, it was all coming together in his head. He would kill Wink without his even seeing it coming, and then they would be even. He watched as Wink opened the back door on the passenger side and grabbed a gym bag and pair of sneakers, then walked up the steps and back inside.

"Mom, why you crying?" asked Wink, as he saw his sisters, Leslee and Linda, consoling their mother as she sat on the living room sofa, weeping.

"That boy killed Jeremy, that boy killed him...just took my son," she bellowed.

The woman's emotions took over, and she continued to cry. "And now he's gone. Now he's gone..."

Wink couldn't stand to see his mother cry. But, ever since the death of Jeremy it seemed that crying had become a regular pattern for her, and he couldn't take it anymore. He knew what had to be done, if nothing else, for his mother's pain, so his brother wouldn't have died in vain, and for his own peace, he'd show Nard what it felt like to hurt someone's family the way that Nard had hurt his.

Vivian left the doctor's office. Her fear of stomach cancer had been unfounded. Her secretary's bright idea was now a reality. And it was now a documented fact that she was indeed pregnant and was definitely having a baby. *We have to get married*, she thought to herself. *What am I going to do? What is Tommy going to say?* The truth was it would kill her mother. Marceline Lang would die a thousand deaths if any of her daughters came home pregnant, or worse came home pregnant without a husband.

"A woman doesn't do these things. A woman just doesn't let these kinds of things happen. Whatever you do, don't ever go too far. There's only so far you can go, then before you know it, oops, you've gone too far and then you end up with a baby before the husband. What kind of life is that? Listen to your mother and trust me; don't have sex until you're married."

Vivian could picture her mother's face, and the words coming out of her mother's mouth.

"Jesus Christ, Vivian, if I told you once I told you a thousand times. What the hell is wrong with you? Why would you get pregnant by him? He's a scumbag! Of all the men in the world, my God, look at who you picked to mate with. What's wrong with you?"

Vivian's family didn't care for Tommy any more than Tommy's family cared for her.

"It's bad enough you're a fucking cop, Tommy, you'd think you'd stay clear of the FBI, but not you, you got to go and fuck an agent?" his little brother, Sammy, teased him one day.

"You see the fucking rack on her, come on, FBI my ass, she's hot, and her tits, oh, my God, you should see her tits, oh, my god, you should fuck her, then you'd understand," he responded, as if he was so serious he could have died of a heart attack right then and there.

"Her fucking rack is gonna have us all sitting behind bars. Wake up, why don't you!"

But love has a way of doing strange things and before anyone could stop them, they were living together, and now they were having a baby.

REASONABLE DOUBT

Day Three

Tommy rolled over as he began to wake from a good night's sleep. Vivian was lying on her side, her back to him. She was still asleep. He leaned on her, taking her body in his arm and caressing her breast as he buried his head in her neck. She felt him moving his hand down her stomach to her legs as he rubbed between them.

"Ohh, Tommy."

"I'm going to fuck the shit out of you," he whispered, spreading her legs open as he mounted behind her. She hadn't completely awakened, but then again, he didn't need her to. She gave him what he wanted, never saying no, even when she wasn't in the mood. Luckily that was never.

"Ohh, Tommy, fuck me, fuck me harder," she said as he stroked her, now on his feet, banging her out doggie style. That's how she got it, every morning. He squeezed her hips, squeezing his hands into her hip bones, thrusting in and out of her, moving her the way he wanted. He pulled his dick out, quickly reinserting it into her ass, fucking her like a virtual reality doll.

"Tommy, please, Tommy," she said as he came inside her before collapsing on top of her.

A Channel 10 news reporter was standing outside the Catholic church, reporting the finding of another abandoned baby.

"Oh jeez...you got to be kidding me," said Vivian as she rolled over in Tommy's bed.

"What," asked Tommy, his heart pounding, wondering if she knew he had snuck out in the middle of the night.

"Another baby. I just got handed that bank robbery case and the abandoned church baby case yesterday," she said, sitting up and watching as the news reporter interviewed Sister Catherine, the nun who had discovered the baby early this morning.

Tommy's heart dropped when he heard her mention the bank robbery case. He turned his head and looked at her watching the news. *Nah, nothing, don't even mention it.*

Tommy picked the remote off the nightstand, breathing a deep sigh as he sat down on the edge of his bed. Vivian reached over and began rubbing his back. The Channel 10 news crew flashed and was now in front of City Hall. Today would be the start of a very long and very newsworthy day. Not only did the city of Philadelphia have a string of babies being abandoned all over town, the Somerset murder case had now taken a completely new turn.

"It now appears that in as little as twenty-four hours Bernard Guess, who had been pinned as a vicious murderer and was facing life in prison, is now looking more and more like an innocent victim who needs to be rescued from persecution. Closing arguments in this case are scheduled to begin at nine this morning. Who knows, the city might have a verdict as early as this afternoon or this evening, Renee. Don't worry, I'll keep you posted. This is Bob Daskins reporting live for Channel 10 news."

"Get the fuck outta here!" said Tommy, throwing the remote at the television.

"Tommy, what the hell? You're going to break the television," said Vivian, looking at the remote control he had just thrown lying on the floor. "Nice," she said, shaking her head in dismay.

"Shut up, Viv," said Tommy before he picked up the battery back of the remote and two batteries and laid them on the dresser, ignoring her as he went back to the bathroom.

"They're gonna let this fucking guy off, Viv! I can't believe this shit. Why the fuck do I even waste my time chasing down these fucking scumbag criminals if they're just going to let them go, scot-free. You gotta be kidding me. Fuck me!"

"Yeah, see, we don't have those kinds of problems where I work," she joked, her reference to working for the FBI completely ignored. "If we come for you, you're going to prison, usually for a long, long, time in what we call penitentiaries."

"Closing arguments my ass, I gotta get down to the courthouse."

Beverly awoke to the sound of the phone ringing. She reached over a pillow, patted the top of the nightstand, and fumbled with the receiver before picking up the phone.

"Hello," she whispered. It was a friend of the family calling about a party she was invited to.

Beverly wrote down the woman's number, promising to call her back, before disconnecting the call.

She peeled back the bed covers, exposing the naked ass of her boyfriend, Tyrone.

"Come on, now, it's cold," he fussed as he threw the covers back over his head.

"I got to go, I forgot all about court," said Beverly.

"Court, what you going there for?" said Tyrone, eyes shut, still half asleep.

"What you think? My son is on trial and closing arguments is today," said Beverly as she cupped her perfect size Cs in their holder and fastened her bra around her back.

I know she not messing up perfectly good sleep for that no-good sorry-ass don't know what the hell to call him son of hers.

She slipped her legs into a skirt and put on a button-down top, looking more professional than most working women with a nine to five. "You act like you don't know what's going on."

"I wish you had told me that shit, I could have stayed at my momma's house last night and got some damn sleep," he said groggily, planting his two feet on the floor, scratching his head with one hand and his groin with the other.

"What?" he asked wondering why she was staring at him.

"I forgot. I'm sorry. Come on, I got to go," she said, ready to throw him outside, his clothes right behind him.

"Shit, man, you fucking me all up," said Tyrone, still not fully awake.

"No, you fucking yourself up, now come on, I got to go," she mumbled from the bathroom while brushing her teeth. She walked down the hall, knocked on the door to Nard's room, making sure Crystal was up and ready.

Tyrone pulled on his pants and threw on his shirt. He put on his socks and his sneakers and grabbed his jacket from the back of a chair.

"You ready?" asked Beverly as she finished combing her hair, looking at Tyrone in frustration.

"Man, don't worry about me, is you ready?"

"Come on, you gotta go," she said, ushering him out of her

bedroom, wondering why she even bothered with him. "You get on my nerves, you know that, right?" she asked as they made their way down the flight of steps to the first floor.

"Hey, Mr. Guess," said Tyrone, showing respect to the old head as he made his way out the door. "Call me when you done," he hollered at Beverly.

"All right," she said as she fumbled with a bottle of high-blood-pressure pills her uncle was suppose to take twice a day.

"He's a fool if I ever seen one in my life," said Uncle Ray Ray, referring to Tyrone. "A goat," he added, spooning a teaspoon of sugar into his morning cup of coffee. "What's that story, the girl with the goats?" he asked calmly, his brain working slowly this early in the morning. "Heidi, that's it," he said, laughing. 'Cause you is a goat herder with that nigga right there. Heidi," he said now in a full robust laughter.

"Dag, Uncle Ray Ray, I can't get the cap off," she said as she read the safety warning, completely ignoring him. "Oh, here it is."

"Ignore me all you want to, Heidi," he said, still laughing at the very thought of Tyrone.

She handed him the pills and then made two slices of toast with grape jelly before passing him some cream.

"Good morning Uncle Ray Ray," said Crystal, making her way through the kitchen carrying nine-month-old Dayanna on her hip.

"Yeah, good morning to you," he answered, being as polite as he was going to be this morning.

"This the last day of the trial, closing arguments today, Uncle Ray Ray."

"I don't know what to say about that boy," Uncle Ray Ray retorted, feeling sorry for the youngster. "You know these young people today don't make much sense to me," he said, looking at Beverly as she slipped on a pair of black heels and her jacket. "Look at Bernard, he could have been anything he wanted to be, but he wanted to run in them streets and be a gangster. Now, he's facing life in prison. Just don't make no sense, no sense at all."

"All right then, I'll be back in a few hours," she added, a little louder.

Ray Ray looked up from his cup of coffee, wishing Beverly would stop talking so loudly. All she was doing was yapping. He could hardly hear the television.

"Uncle Ray Ray, did you hear me, make sure you take your pills, too," she added, watching him mosey into the living room.

"Dagnabbit! I told you, I told you," he said, pointing at the game show host on the television.

Beverly stopped and looked at the television monitor at a young woman who was jumping up and down for joy.

"Did you hear me, Uncle Ray Ray? You got to make sure you take your medication."

"I sure do wish you'd go on somewhere," said Uncle Ray Ray, now clapping and laughing at the television.

"I got your go somewhere," mumbled Beverly as she opened the door, letting Crystal and the baby pass. They walked to the corner and hopped the bus, which was visible from two blocks away. It was a dreary, chilly fall day, and it had begun to rain just as soon as she parked the car. Beverly pulled her jacket hood over her head and made her way to the front entrance of the courthouse. She zipped through security and rushed upstairs to the fourth floor. She opened the left side of the heavy wooded double doors. Judge Means's courtroom was packed. She walked inside and took a seat next to Crystal and the baby. She looked at her best friend, Donna, seated on the other side of Crystal.

"Don't worry, it'll work out," whispered Donna, as if she had been given a sign from God and could predict the future.

The district attorney was already on his feet. As Beverly settled into her seat, she heard him directing the jury to find her son guilty. He kept repeating that the only person one could blame for the deaths of Jeremy Tyler and Lance Robertson was Bernard Guess, as it was his gun that had killed both of them. However, the jury had technically already heard that story when Nard took the stand claiming self-defense, and then his lawyer, Bobby DeSimone, backed his theory with hardcore evidence of the break-in. After Zone finished his closing argument, Bobby DeSimone took to the floor. His demeanor was confident and sure. He had everything he needed to remind the jury that they could not find his client guilty of murder in the first degree, and with the way things looked, he could possibly get the kid off altogether based on the claim of self-defense.

"Ladies and gentlemen of the jury, the state has done a wonderful job of wasting our time in this courtroom," he said, indicating Zone, seated to his right. "And all this time was wasted attempting to prove a double homicide occurred on the night in question. However, that simply is not fact and it certainly is not the case. As we clearly proved to you, my client was left with no options by the hands of two intruders with loaded handguns. And while the state would have you think differently, you can't, because the evidence clearly shows the truth. Remember when you go back in that room, you have a young kid's life at stake. The state has a job to do, they are suppose to prove to you beyond a reasonable doubt that my client murdered those men in cold blood, and, you know what, ladies and gentlemen?" he said, spinning around and pointing his finger at them, staring each in the eye. "They just haven't done that."

DeSimone smoothly turned around and strolled back to his table. If he wasn't in a court of law he'd smack high fives with Nard himself.

"We got 'em, you're gonna be all right, kid," whispered DeSimone as the judge gave out instructions. The courtroom watched as the jury rose before deliberating.

It was 10:21 and DeSimone wanted a cup of coffee. "I'm going downstairs, don't worry, kid, they won't be too long."

"You think they'll make a decision before the day's out?" Nard asked hopefully, as the sheriff came to cuff him and escort him into the back holding area.

"I think they're gonna make a decision in the next hour." DeSimone smiled, winking at Nard.

DeSimone had barely taken his first sip of coffee before the vibration of his pager caught his attention. He reached in his jacket pocket and looked at the number of his office. He went over to the pay phone and called Sandra, his secretary.

"They're ready," she said, hearing his hello.

"The verdict's in on the Somerset case already?"

"That's what they called and said," she said, a slight hint of aggravation in her voice.

"Great." He hung up the phone, went back over to the tiny newsstand inside the courthouse, placed fifty cents on the counter for his cup of coffee, and headed back upstairs.

It had only been thirty-five minutes that the jury had deliberated. The case didn't need a group of rocket scientists to conjure up a verdict, DeSimone had made sure of that. He had done his job, and Zone; well, let's just say that in DeSimone's opinion, Zone had put all his eggs in one basket, a stripper named Daisy Mae Fothergill, and thought he had an ace in the hole, but he was terribly wrong. DeSimone flipped the tables on the courtroom, fed the jury what they needed to hear so they could give him what he wanted—a not guilty verdict—and that's exactly what had happened.

"Have you reached a verdict?" asked Judge Means, peering over the frame of his reading glasses as he questioned the foreman responsible for reading the verdict to the courtroom.

"Yes we have, Your Honor," said the colored man now standing, reading a three-by-five index card in his hand. "On the charge of murder in the first degree of Lance Robertson, we find the defendant not guilty. On the charge of manslaughter, we, the jury, find the defendant guilty." The foreman then sat down as the courtroom began to buzz with the finding.

"Sentencing will take place in two weeks, counsel, you'll be notified of a date, court is adjourned!" The judge banged his gavel, rose from his chair, and walked off the stand, through a door, and into the back offices.

"Yes!" exclaimed DeSimone as he hugged Nard. "This is great, just great. I told you, you'd be okay. Do you fucking believe it, even with the girl turning state and testifiying against you, we still won!" DeSimone was so elated he couldn't help but hug Nard again. Nard, on the other hand, didn't seem too happy.

"What, kid, ain't you happy?"

"Manslaughter? They still found me guilty," he said, feeling as if all was lost.

"Yeah, but, kid, trust me, the district attorney's office charged you with murder one. You beat a murder one charge, we got it down to manslaughter and aggravated assault, what's wrong with you? Nard you still have your life." DeSimone didn't care if he sat for the next couple of years, as far as he was concerned, the case was a win. Nard wouldn't be spending the rest of his life locked behind bars. Instead, he'd spend three, maybe five years tops in a state correctional facility. DeSimone didn't understand why he wasn't happy. "You got the best deal you could've gotten, kid, the absolute best."

Behind him, Nard could hear his girlfriend and his mother. He turned around and smiled at Beverly, who couldn't hold back tears of joy.

"You coming home, baby," said Donna, waving her fist in the air as she hugged Beverly, who felt faint at the sound of the words.

His girlfriend, Crystal, hugged their baby, Dayanna, smiling and waving the baby's hand at him.

Wink and his family silently rose from the back of the courtroom, making their way out the double wooded doors and into the corridor. Wink turned around and looked at Nard's family hugging one another and jumping for joy. *It ain't over, nigga, you'll see, an eye for an eye, motherfucker.*

Lester Giles's wife, Euretha, followed behind them. The verdict didn't affect her as did the loss or better yet, gain, of Lester. However, she followed it through like she was supposed to; after all, Lester was her husband.

Lucille Davis exited the courtroom not far behind. She couldn't move as fast as some of the other people, but she slowly took her time and filed out the double doors of the courtroom.

Lance's mother, who hadn't missed one day of the trial, also followed the line of folks out the door. She, too, being an older lady, a single mother of two, took in the testimony of Bernard Guess and listened with remorse at what her son had been accused of. And to think, the man who took her son's life had beaten the murder case. Justice, for her, had no name. The trial had taken its toll and the truth of her son being a would-be burglar lay heavy and brought her heart a sea of emotions. The thought of raising a son who would turn out to be a cold-blooded murderer was too much for her to bear. Ms. Robertson had no intention of returning to the courtroom, even though the defense attorney had asked her to be present at the sentencing and wanted her on the stand to speak on behalf of her son. She didn't think she could do it. What could she say that would make a difference? She honestly believed there was nothing more that should be said. Now, thank God, it was done and over and everybody could just put it all behind them.

Tommy Delgado and Merva Ross watched as the courtroom dispersed. He walked toward the front of the courtroom, an uneasy smile spread across his face.

"What the hell happened? That guy is just gonna walk, scot-free?" said Delgado, not so much angry as he was disappointed and ready to pounce all over Zone. Ross held his arm, making sure her partner didn't end up in trouble.

"What can I say? I thought we had it. I was wrong. Once we had the girl, and her testimony, I assumed the case was in the bag. Look, I know you guys work hard out there, risking your lives to keep the streets safe, but we can't win them all, right?" Zone shrugged, not really caring one way or another.

His disconnect was apparent and Tommy faded for a moment back to the house on Somerset Street, to where the bodies of Saunta Davis and her son, DaShawn, lay sprawled in pools of blood, the little boy already dead, the mother barely breathing.

"Come on, Delgado, you see it every day out there, right. They just keep killing each other," Zone said, a confused look on his face. "Don't worry, we'll get 'em next time," he quickly added, patting Tommy on the shoulder as he grabbed his briefcase off the rectangular table and headed toward the doors. He knew the media would be waiting for him. Win or lose, he still got his name in the paper.

"Yeah, next time, you fucking piece of shit, why don't you do your fucking job," Tommy muttered to himself before he and Merva walked out the doors of the courtroom to a pack of thirsty reporters.

As usual, Liddles was parked in back of the lot across from City Hall. Karla-Jae crossed the street, got into the van, and reported of the events in the courtroom to her brother as she usually did.

"He beat the case after all," sighed Liddles.

Liddles's smile spoke a thousand words. He was glad Nard beat the case for killing the guys who were responsible for killing his brother. But, even with justice playing her merciful part, it wasn't enough. Poncho was still gone, his mother's heart was still broken, and his pain was no less.

Liddles had spent every day following Wink. Like a peeping Tom, he was watching carefully. Wink could forget about it. Liddles had Wink's entire itinerary, drug house, drug stash, baby momma's crib, baby momma's job, momma's home, momma's job, sister's school, brother's wife's mother's cousin's house, the whole family had been scoped out.

Then there was the other one, Lance Robertson, Jeremy Tyler's cohort. It turned out, Lance was a loner of sorts, and the only family he had was his mom's, Mrs. Robertson, and Liddles already had her ammo. He knew where she worked, where she went to school, what time she ate dinner, what time she left the house every day. He had followed her enough to know how and when to make a move on her if he wanted to. She was a goner, too. Any of them could be got and would be. It was all a matter of timing. When it was all said and done, they would wish they had never laid one finger on his brother, Poncho's head.

Wink, on the other hand, was ready to spit fire. He was so heated, he couldn't contain his anger.

"How the fuck they gonna let this nigga off like that?" asked a troubled Wink. His anger was getting the best of him. He could no longer contain himself. The only comfort he had was knowing that no matter where Nard went, he could be got in prison. Wink had family throughout Pennsylvania's prison system, and wherever Nard was sent to do his time, there would be people on the inside waiting to take him out.

"Wink, calm down," said Leslee, trying to get Wink to sit with her on the sofa.

"Leslee, that fucking judge and jury let that nigga walk, they let him walk," said Wink, unable to believe the verdict and unable to believe that Nard was getting off with a slap on the wrist manslaughter charge. "He'll be home in less than five for manslaughter. That's nothing after what he did to my brother."

"Wink, just calm down."

"No, I won't calm down. We'll see. This nigga thinks he's going to get away with killing my brother, that shit just ain't gonna happen," Wink said, picking up his nine-millimeter and making sure his clip was fully loaded.

"Where you going?" asked Leslee, scared of her brother and what he might do.

"I'm gonna show that motherfucker, Nard, how it feels to have his family fucked with, that's what I'm going to do," said Wink as he stuffed the gun in his hoodie and slammed the front door behind him.

"The social worker's bringing me another baby. All the paperwork is complete and there's nothing really left for them to do," said Donna, quickly adding, "I'm getting one of them abandoned babies and the news is coming so you got to watch Channel 10 tonight."

"For real?" asked Beverly, truly amazed Donna would be interviewed on the evening news.

"Wow, Donna, this is big." Beverly smiled, then added, "You hear that, Uncle Ray Ray? Donna's gonna be on the evening news."

"That's really something. And they interviewing you?" he said, shaking his head at the shame of it all.

"Yeah, you know, only a crazy person would abandon a baby like that." She sighed, not understanding what kind of person would leave a baby in the cold.

"They pay good money?" asked Beverly, thinking about getting her a foster child, too.

"Girl, they pay real good money, but you know, you get more for the handicapped ones," she said, serious as a heart attack.

"How much more?" asked Beverly.

"I don't know, 'cause I ain't got time for no motherfucker can't walk and talk and shit," she said, biting into a piece of fried chicken. "But, it's a lot more, girl, a lot."

"And the state be giving these children to you?" asked Uncle Ray Ray, as if he needed to write a strongly worded letter to the Department of Human Services.

"Yeah, and?"

"Shit, when they find out, this shit liable to be on the evening news and not you."

"Look, I'm good to them children, where would they be without me?"

"Probably living with a kind family who would be taking proper care of them and not pocketing state assistance for Jheri curl money," said Ray Ray, knowing he was starting trouble, as he liked to.

"Don't worry about my Jheri curl, Ray," she said, fluffing her

Jheri curl mane, looking like Michael Jackson back in the day. "Look, my kids wouldn't be nowhere if it wasn't for me," she said, lighting a Newport. "Shit, I don't see you in here making a difference in a child's life, Ray!" she snapped.

"I don't see you making no difference neither," he teased her back.

"Shut up," she said, blowing a spitball from her mouth that she had sat there and rolled between her fingers from a torn corner of a piece of napkin.

"I bet the SPCA won't even let you have a cat. You know god damn well, she done tricked them people into giving her them kids," he said to his niece, shaking his head as if it really was a shame.

"You know, your uncle gets on my nerves," Donna said as she kissed her friend good-bye.

"Bye, Ray," she said, walking past him and out the door.

"Bye yourself," he said, watching her twitching her ass from side to side as Beverly closed and locked the door.

"Them people is crazy paying Donna all that good money. I feel sorry for them poor babies. Damn, they need they families bad," noted Uncle Ray Ray as he sat down in his favorite chair to watch television.

Everything was working out for Beverly and her family. Even though Nard was going to prison, his lawyer said he didn't expect him to serve more than a three-year sentence. That was a far cry from the rest of his life.

She finished dinner and took Uncle Ray Ray's plate and set it in the sink.

A banging sound at the door broke her reverie.

"Coming," she said. Looking out a square window in the middle of the door, she saw her cousin Chris.

"Hey, cousin, is my dad here?"

"Umm, yeah, come on in. He's in the living room," said Beverly as she led Chris down the hall.

The three of them filled Chris in on the trial and the verdict.

Beverly made some apple cinnamon spice tea and told him all the details of the trial as they sipped tea in the living room.

Chris was Uncle Ray Ray's son, and he and Beverly had grown up together. She could remember many days playing endlessly with her cousins as a young child growing up. Her father, Benjamin Guess, whom everyone lovingly called Benny, had died, and Uncle Ray Ray shortly thereafter needed a place to stay. Having four sons didn't help his situation, as none of his own children were in a position to care for him. And unfortunately, they could barely take care of themselves. Raymond, Jr., his oldest, was currently serving time in prison. And Ralph was living with his girlfriend in her mother's basement. Charlie was shacked up with his girlfriend of fifteen years. And while he owned his home and was the only one out of the four who had his life together, he had no room or ability to care for his father. His girlfriend, Karen, came with two children, and over the past fifteen years, she had managed to have six more, for a total of eight kids, who were worse than Bey Bey kids themselves. And then there was Chris, the youngest of Uncle's Ray's children, and while everyone believed he had turned out to be the most promising, no one had yet discovered that Chris had developed a terrible addiction to smoking cocaine.

"Jesus, Lord almighty, I don't know what to say," he said, shaking his head as he sat down in his favorite recliner, looking at his lottery tickets. "It's always something, ain't that girl supposed to be staying here? What's her name, with that baby she got?"

"Crystal?" asked Beverly, knowing who he was speaking of.

"Yeah, that's the one."

"She said she was going to get some more clothes and would be back later on."

"Lord have mercy, that baby of hers just cries all night long."

"Really, I heard nothing."

"Umm, Dad, can I talk to you for a minute in the kitchen?" asked Chris, his adrenaline pumping at the thought of getting some money in his sweaty palms.

"Whatever it is that you want to talk about doesn't have anything to do with my money, does it?" asked Uncle Ray Ray, just about tired of Chris taking his pocket money. "'Cause if it is, I don't think we need to be conversating no more."

Before Chris could speak, the front door opened and Crystal made her way inside, toting the baby, a baby bag, and a small duffel bag filled with more of her things.

"I'm here," she called out in the foyer.

"We're in here," called out Beverly from the living room.

Uncle Ray Ray got up out of his chair to follow Chris into the kitchen, just as a bullet shattered the living room window, followed by a second, then a third, and what appeared to be a shower of gunfire, a barrage of bullets spraying the house.

"Oh, my God!" screamed Crystal, holding the baby.

"GET DOWN!" yelled Uncle Ray Ray, immediately dropping to the floor. "GET DOWN ON THE FLOOR, NOW!"

Everyone's instincts for safety seemed to follow Uncle Ray Ray's command and they all ducked for safety behind walls, furniture, and whatever they could. Chris dove into the kitchen headfirst like a runner diving for home plate. Crystal fell to the floor, her baby screaming as she cupped her underneath her body as best she could. Uncle Ray Ray slithered behind his trusty recliner, and just as the bullets stopped, a car engine could be heard as tires screeched down the block.

"Beverly, you okay?" asked Uncle Ray Ray, noticing that Beverly was still sitting upright on the sofa as if nothing had happened. Ray saw the whites of her eyes as they shut, and then, slowly, she slumped to the side and rolled off the sofa and onto the floor. The first bullet that had come through the left window had grazed the back of her head as the bullet passed her, piercing the wall behind her. Beverly never had a chance to take cover. The only thing that saved her was angle and location. A few more inches to the right and Beverly would have been shot in the center of the head. The second bullet hit her in the back above her shoulder blade, lodging inside.

"Beverly!" Uncle Ray Ray yelled. He got up quickly and ran over to her side as everyone in the house could hear the drive-by's tires screeching down the block.

"Oh, my God!" screamed Crystal, still cradling a crying Dayanna through all the commotion.

"Call 911!" yelled Uncle Ray Ray to Chris, who was standing there in shock. "Call 911, I said, don't just stand there," he yelled at his son again. The sight of blood stopped Chris dead in his tracks and he couldn't move. All he could see was the dark black blood soaking his father's shirt.

"Chris, call 911, I said!" Uncle Ray Ray hollered as Crystal, still cradling a screaming baby, dialed 911.

"I need an ambulance, Ms. Beverly's been shot, please, please send somebody quick, I don't think she's breathing, she don't look like she's breathing," screamed a sobbing Crystal, her nerves shaking as she nervously held the phone and spoke to the 911 operator. Of course the 911 operator began to ask a series of questions, and Crystal could be heard answering with a series of I don't knows.

"Is they sending an ambulance?" questioned Uncle Ray Ray, holding Beverly in his arms.

"Yeah, the lady says one is coming, it's on the way."

"Chris, what the hell you standing there for like a frozen statue? Boy, get your ass upstairs and get me some towels out the closet. We got to do something to try and stop all this bleeding," said Ray Ray, covered in the dark black blood that was coming from his niece's head wound and the back of her shoulder.

It would be another fifteen minutes and two more 911 calls before the police or an ambulance would arrive. But finally, they stormed into the house all at the same time. Uncle Ray Ray broke down at the sight of the paramedics preparing Beverly's body for transport. The room fell silent as they gently lifted her body onto the gurney and rolled her into the back of an ambulance.

"Don't let her die, God. Don't let her die," Crystal whispered between sobs. A bloody Ray Ray answered a few questions before being offered a ride to Temple Hospital. The entire block was standing outside, eyewitnesses to all the commotion.

"Don't worry, Ray, she'll be all right," shouted Clarence from his porch. Ray just waved his hand at everybody. *I sure do hope so.*

Tommy and Vivian were seated in the back of Carmen's, an Italian restaurant located down in South Philly. Carmen Pangione had been in the food business all his life. He started with a small hoagie shop called Rocco's. He invented the chicken a la Rocco's hoagie and sold them all day long in the Reading Terminal Market, making himself a very rich man.

"Hey, guys, good to see you two. How you been, Tommy, how's the family?" asked Carmen as he greeted them both, hugging and kissing Vivian, then doing the same to Tommy.

"Everybody's good, Carmen, how's everybody doing? How's your wife and kids?"

"Everybody's wonderful. You want a bottle of wine, let me get you something real nice, on the house," he said, patting Tommy on the back. "Get my friends here a bottle of water for their table," he ordered as he rushed off to his wine cellar to fetch a real good year. Within a matter of minutes he was back holding two round wineglasses and a bottle of Fontalloro Felsina in his hand. "For you, Tommy, anything you need, you just let me know."

"Thanks, Carmen," said Tommy nonchalantly, as if the extra-nice treatment were completely normal.

"Wow, now he gets an A plus for service, I'd say," chimed Vivian.

"An old friend of my family," said Tommy. "He watched me grow up. You know how it is," assured Tommy. "Trust me, as long as I've known Carmen, that guy will be dancing at my wedding with bells on," smiled Tommy.

Vivian thought of her wedding day. He did say he'd get the ring. Then again, maybe this is all too soon for him. Maybe he can't handle all this. Maybe I shouldn't tell him about the baby. But, he needs to know, it's his baby, too.

"What's the matter, you don't like the wine?"

"No, the wine is delicious. It's just that…I have something to tell you and I don't know how to say it."

A waiter quickly set two house salads down in front of them, poured their glasses full of water, and then asked if they were ready to order their main course or if they needed more time.

"I'm ready," replied Tommy, "you?" he asked, looking over at Vivian. Her face said a thousand words, all of which meant "no." "Can we get a few more minutes?" he asked the waiter, who politely bowed his head before walking away.

"What's the matter?"

"It's serious, Tommy, I'm trying to talk to you."

"Viv, I was just ordering dinner, I didn't mean to upset you. Come on, tell me what's bothering you."

"Are you sure you want to know?"

"Vivian, you're killing me over here, come on."

"I'm pregnant, Tommy. We're going to have a baby."

He was silent as the words traveled through his ears, into his brain, and seeped into the reality of his being. There were many ways to look at the situation. It was good, and in a way it was bad. Bad because he wasn't ready for fatherhood. Dating Vivian, an FBI agent, was scary enough, marriage and baby had him ready to run for the hills. It was way too much responsibility. He wasn't even ready to be responsible for toothpaste, let alone a wife or a child. He could feel himself beginning to perspire, the room closing in, and a wave of anxiety hit him like a wave crashing to shore.

"Tommy are you okay, you look like you can hardly breathe."

He looked at her across the table. She was a good match for him, smart, intelligent, in law enforcement. Her beauty far outweighed her brains, and if you didn't know any better, you would expect Vivian Lang should have been a pinup model on a poster in an auto body shop. She was the ultimate package, but a baby?

"Do you know how lucky you are?" he joked.

"What, what are you talking about? This is totally serious, Tommy."

"And at the end of the day, you got lucky?"

"What does that mean?"

"It means we're going to be family. You need to plan the wedding, right away, 'cause no kid of mine will be born a bastard and not have a father and not have a name. I'm such a stand-up fucking guy. And you're lucky, Vivian, really lucky you caught me when you did."

"Hey, Carmen, we're getting married…and having a baby!"

"Congratulazioni!" he shouted in Italian. *"Celebriamo!"*

PLANS A, B, C, AND D

Liddles parked his car, tucked his gun in his waistband, and with the other hand grabbed an FTD tiger lily arrangement from the front seat. He locked up his dusty old blue van, then walked up the unfamiliar block and into an apartment building behind a young female struggling with several bags of groceries managing two small children.

"Excuse me," he said politely as he passed by and took the corridor in the opposite direction, toward the stairwell. He began climbing, his lean and toned body built for every step of the twelve flights he would have to climb. And even though the apartment building had an elevator, his diversion served its purpose. Actually, everything he had planned for the last six months would now serve its purpose. A well-thought-out and well-planned purpose.

Liddles was and had always been the thinker, one step ahead. He had the quality of patience and used time, unlike others, who wasted it. He had everything figured out before he made a move. He had watched and followed Lance's mother all day. From court to the Septa bus to the corner store, to the apartment building, he had seen it all through his binoculars from the driver's seat of his old dusty blue van as he sat patiently like a jaguar biding time before it attacks its prey.

A little out of breath from the climb and with a rush of pulsating adrenaline from knowing what he was about to do, he knocked at the door. There was no answer so he knocked again and pressed his head closer to the door. He could hear the faint sound of the A Team's theme music playing from the television.

Mrs. Robertson glanced at the dresser as she slipped her housecoat over her head. Mrs. Robertson was a retired schoolteacher from South Philly High. She had worked with young children from second-graders to tenth-graders, teaching and molding them into young adults. She had dedicated her life to her students. Her husband, Fred Robertson, had died from cancer years ago. So, it was just her and her son, Lance. And now that he had been killed in what the media was calling a botched robbery, she had no one except her cat, Boots. She did have a younger sister who lived in New Jersey with her family. But they didn't talk much. Her brother had died years ago, in the 1970s. The police said it was gang-related and had no witnesses or suspects. No arrests were ever made.

She looked at her lottery tickets. *Lucky 147, baby. If I hit, I need so much I don't even know what I'd buy first.*

She heard the bell on Boots's collar jingle as he pranced down the hall, then a wind whispered through the bedroom window. *Let me close this window before I forget and catch cold.* Once she had closed the window and pulled the draperies to and fro so they lay just right, she took a few steps back to examine their timeless beauty. The draperies had been passed down from her momma's momma's momma from out of a real-life plantation in Drew, Mississippi, where her kinfolks were from. Then she heard the faint sound of knocking on the door.

Somebody's at the door, Bootsy. Probably one of them kids from down the hall making noise again.

Then again another knock at the door.

"All right, all right, I'm coming," bellowed Mrs. Robertson. She finished slipping into her housecoat and made her way to the door. She looked out the peephole.

"Who is it?" said a soft gentle voice from behind the door.

"Floral delivery, ma'am," said Liddles, hoping this would prompt her to open the door.

"Flowers, I'm not expecting any flowers," she said as the tiger lilies' orange petals did their job. Liddles could hear the woman unhooking the chain and unlocking the locks. She opened her door and stared into the eyes of the grim reaper himself who had come for her.

Liddles pointed the barrel of a .38 at the elderly woman and closed the door behind him.

"I've been waiting to see…I had a feeling you was coming," she said, already knowing what he was there for. Mrs. Robertson stood still, facing the barrel of the gun dead on. She didn't scream, she wasn't scared, she just wished she had fed her cat, Boots, before her assassin had showed up.

"As I walk through the valley…" she began, her eyes still calmly staring at her fate.

"Don't nobody want to hear that shit, we ain't in no valley, neither. Shut up, turn around, and get down on the floor," Liddles ordered, still standing in the doorway. The woman did as she was told, turned around and bent down as she got on her knees. She felt the heavy metal of the steel gun at the base of her skull.

"I'm sorry for your brother."

Liddles hesitated for one split second…before pulling the

trigger. He watched as the older woman's body leaned against the wall. She fell to the floor, her blood oozing out of the back of her head into a puddle where she lay.

"I'm sorry for my brother, too," he said, speaking back to the dead woman.

He picked up his vase of tiger lilies and closed the door behind him as her cat, Boots, walked over to where she lay. He sniffed the small pile of blood next to her head, let out a soft meow, and sat waiting patiently for his dinner to be served.

"Hey, Delgado, and Ross, get in here. Now!" shouted Captain O'Reilly. "Delgado, what the fuck is going on with you? I hear you're about to be a family man?" asked the captain, patting Tommy on his back, as if he was a proud father.

"Yeah, yeah, yeah, I'm getting married and I'm inviting you to my wedding." Tommy smiled. "You and the chief."

"I wouldn't miss it for the world," he said, before turning to Ross. "Hey, Ross, how's it going with you?" he asked Merva, not wanting her to feel left out of all the small talk.

"I'm good, Captain, everything is well," she retorted.

"That's good to hear. Listen guys, we got two cases I want you to pick up and report back to me pronto. The first is a drive-by on Twenty-third Street off the corner of Susquehanna. Looks like we got a woman in her midforties, shot in the back of the head, in stable condition at Jefferson; her name is Beverly Guess. Take this," said the captain, passing a folder to Merva.

"And the next case I got for the two of you is an old lady, shot and killed in the doorway of her apartment out in West Philadelphia. There was no forcible entry and no one heard a thing, not even the gunshot," he said, passing another folder to Tommy.

"I want the two of you to see what you can come up with,"

he said, hoping they could solve the case before sundown. "The mayor's office wants an arrest, so I need you guys to look sharp out there, you got it?"

"We got it, don't worry about a thing," said Tommy, patting his back.

"We're on it, Captain," added Merva, as she and Tommy walked out of the captain's office, closing his door behind them.

"So, where should we start, old lady or drive-by?" asked Tommy.

Merva pulled a coin out of her pocket. "Heads old lady, tails drive-by," she said as she flicked the coin, caught it, and slapped it on the back of her hand, "Tails! We do the drive-by," she said as she stuffed the coin back in her pocket.

"Tails it is," said Tommy as he held the door for her to walk through.

Arizona State University, Tempe, Arizona

Daisy Mae Fothergill was in the final stages of being relocated and placed into the witness protection program. Her paperwork had been pushed through by none other than Detective Tommy Delgado. And after she testified she was immediately transported to Phoenix, Arizona, where two uniformed officers of the Relocation Unit's specialized services were waiting for her. A woman by the name of Lori Snelling was assigned to Daisy and responsible for her intake. Her job would only last for ninety days and then she'd be out of Daisy's life, forever. But, in the meantime, she would transition Daisy and morph her into her new being. Her job included detail for ninety days, processing Daisy's new identity, home placement, society introduction, job searching, and education, and there was just a ton of paperwork involved for every detail and for every process that Lori was responsible for. But rest assured, when Lori Snelling was done, Daisy Mae Fothergill would no longer exist. She had ninety days and then Lori would be assigned a new case, a new life, a new person to delete from the face of the earth. Some cases required surgery or face-altering. High alert security services were needed in most cases, but not in Daisy's. Lori was confident that Daisy Mae Fothergill would never be found again when she was done.

Daisy remembered how nervous she was at the airport, her first time flying, and now a new place, and a new home, with complete strangers. She had said good-bye to everyone at the courthouse and had nothing familiar from her past except a picture book of her closest friends and relatives. She thought back to the day she had met Lori Snelling.

"Hi, I've been assigned to relocating you. I'll be picking up where Detective Delgado left off. If you have any questions, you are free to ask them. If I have the answers, I will provide them. If I don't, I will get the answers for you." Snelling smiled and helped Daisy with one of her carry-ons. "First, we will go to your hotel and check you in. I will explain the security detail that has been assigned," she said, noticing the frown that appeared on Daisy's face. "No, no, it's just preliminary, all this is, just to get you started and on your way. We'll be out of your hair in no time," Lori said, raising her eyebrows and showing a confident smile.

"What's no time?" asked Daisy, wondering how long no time would actually be.

"We got ninety days, and until then, let's just say, I'm sort of like your shadow. The good thing, though, is if you need me, I'll be right here. But, first things first, I need a name, a new name; that's the only thing Detective Delgado didn't fill in," requested

Lori, just wanting to get the ball rolling.

"A name?" asked Daisy, never having thought of what she wanted to be called.

"Sleep on it, let me know tomorrow. For the night, you'll be in Motel 8, but once we get you situated you'll be in your dorm, a regular 'ol college student like everyone else. Sounds like a lot of fun." Lori Snelling smiled as if it was just the greatest thing in the world.

"College, no one said anything about college."

"Detective Delgado pushed your paperwork. These are his instructions. Your new residence, courtesy of the state of Pennsylvania, is at Arizona State."

Okay, Mr. Detective, since you signed me up for college you can sign me out. Daisy couldn't wait to get to a phone, boy, oh, boy, was she going tear into him when she did, and as soon as Lori closed the crappy Motel 8 door behind her, Daisy picked up the phone and called Tommy.

"Why am I in a Motel 8, and why did you enroll me in college?"

"Well, you have to do something, and there are people in place to keep an eye out for you. You'll be fine. You'll do great."

"I need a job," said Daisy defiantly.

"Doing what? You have no schooling. What, you gonna go back to stripping?"

His question hurt her feelings, because he was saying it to do so and at the same time using her life against her.

"I did what I had to do!" she barked back.

"Okay, fine, now do what you need to do. It's a great opportunity. I want you to make it out here, Daisy. I don't want you to end up dead, you hear me, lying in the fucking gutter somewhere!" He caught his anxiety, his frustration, his hostility, and he remembered what his district's psychiatrist told him to do and quietly counted to four and the anger was gone. He was in control. "Listen, Daisy, you can do this. I know you're scared, but just give it a try. I hooked you up with Lori, isn't she great?"

"Yeah," Daisy sighed with a hint of sarcasm.

"What you say? I can't hear you, speak up," Tommy shot back at her, figuring she needed to be bossed around, just like any other woman he had ever dealt with.

"I said yeah, she's just great, she's the best."

"Okay, so you got away with a nice little stash," said Tommy, knowing all about the arrangement Vivian had made, because he was the one behind it.

"How'd you know about that?"

"Ah, hah, hah, don't you want to know." Tommy joked and teased, but he was really serious, and she would do what he said like everybody else. He knew that if she didn't go, she would limit her chances of surviving, and so far in life, the odds weren't stacked in her favor.

"Hey, just promise me you'll give it a chance."

"Yeah, I'll give it a chance."

"Okay, and one more thing, Daisy."

"What?"

"I'm betting on you, all my money is on you. I know you can do this."

That was two weeks ago, the night they had flown her in. And as scared as she was, she went along for the unknown ride. Lori Snelling turned out to be one of the nicest people Daisy would ever meet, caring, passionate, and understanding.

The two bonded in an unbelievable way. It wasn't hard to understand, though. Lori was from a small town in Oklahoma. One night after her seventeen-year-old sister had a fight with their parents, Lil' Lori, as everyone called her, watched her sister pack a backpack, even though her parents had told her she could not spend the night over her girlfriend's house.

"But it's just a slumber party," she defended, begging like a hungry homeless person. But it didn't work, the Snellings were relentless and they never budged. After the house was quiet and everyone asleep, Christy tiptoed downstairs and came back into the room wearing her jacket.

"Where you going?" Lori asked a fuming Christy.

"I don't know, but far, far, far away from here, that's for sure. I hate it here and I hate them. They never let me do anything. I'm going out."

"Are you coming back tomorrow?" asked Lil' Lori, hoping her sister would say no and that she was leaving for good so she could have her room.

Lori watched as her sister fell silent, opening the window.

"I wish never," said Christy as she climbed out of the window and jumped off the ledge.

"Well, can I have your Madonna poster off your wall?" pint-size nine-year-old Lori asked her seventeen-year-old sister from the window.

"No, don't be dumb," Christy snapped in her usual valley girl snobbish way. "Close the window and be quiet."

That was the last time anyone ever saw Christine Allison Snelling. Her family would be forever broken. Her mother would have a nervous breakdown and her father wouldn't speak for months. She was believed to have been abducted. It was because of her sister that Lori ventured into law enforcement. And to this day, she still searched, hoping to find her long-lost sister.

"Knock knock, you ready, time for school," joked Lori as she opened the door to the hotel room where Daisy was staying.

"I'm ready as I'll ever be," said Daisy, next to her bags.

"It'll be great. Don't worry, you're going to love it. Did you decide on a name?"

"No…well, sort of."

"Well, maybe for you the admissions line will be long today, but you have to figure something by the time we get there."

A name was important because it identified you to the world. A name was also supposed to fit a person like a glove.

Daisy had a *People* magazine on a tabletop with Princess Diana gracing the cover. She was beautiful and regal and her life appeared perfect, loving, and safe. All her life since she was a little girl Daisy had dreamed of being a princess, playing with her dolls and acting as if she herself were royalty. She smiled at the kind face on the page smiling slightly at her. Then there was the challenge of a last name. Channeling her mother, only one came to life, Poitier, after Sidney Poitier, her mother's favorite actor in all the world.

"Diana Abigail Poitier," said Daisy, smiling.

"Wow, great name," said Lori as she started gathering Daisy's luggage and began helping her to the car with it.

The college campus was thirteen miles from Phoenix, Arizona. On the way over, while Lori finished up the paperwork with Daisy's new name, Daisy stared out the window in silence, thinking about everything she had been through. Her life had taken a dramatic turn that involved many lost lives. Her life was certainly a mess, to say the least, and while she couldn't change what had happened in the past, she promised herself that there would be some changes moving forward. The vast green countryside promised a new beginning filled with new possibilities.

Once on campus, Lori Snelling handled everything for Daisy. All she had to do was sit back and smile.

"Wow, you'll be staying in McClintock Hall, and here's your Arizona State Welcome Kit, your key to your room, your school schedule, a booklet and directory of the campus, your counselor's booklet, whom you really need to let help you, and here you go, a welcome bag with all kinds of goodies. Make sure you look at that school schedule folder, because it will let you know all the books you will need to purchase for your classes."

Lori stood over Daisy, passing her folder after folder, welcome kits, and bags of assorted goods, and when she was done, Daisy held a pile at least eight inches thick.

"Wow, that's a lot, but you can handle it, I know you can. Go through everything and remember your counselor can really help guide you until you learn your way."

"Thanks, Lori," said Daisy, truly appreciating all that Lori had done for her over the past two weeks. She hadn't just done her job, she had become a big sister, a mentor, a confidante for Daisy, and Daisy began to feel insecure at the thought of her leaving.

"What will I do without you?" asked Daisy, tears in her eyes at the thought of being alone and having absolutely no one in her life.

"Awww shucks, bumblebee, are you getting sentimental? Not you, city mouse with a heart of steel. Now you're gonna be just fine, Daisy…I mean Diana." She smiled, pointing out Daisy's new name. "I don't even question it. This is a new start and you can't go forward if you stay in the past. Let everything go, and embrace the adventure of your new freedom, your new life, and don't be afraid, just don't be afraid."

"But…I have no one in this world. I'm like the most alone person on the planet."

"No, trust me, you're not, there's people way lonelier than you, believe you me. Listen, there are thousands of young people on this campus trying to figure out who they are, where they belong in life, and what their purpose is. Everyone wants to make friends. Trust me, there's someone here dying to be your friend. I bet in less than a month, you'll have plenty of friends. Really, you're a pretty girl, and you're gonna make friends with no problem. And besides, I'm here and I'm your friend, and I'm only a phone call away," she said, giving Daisy a warm hug, letting her know she wasn't alone. "Trust me, you're not alone. It's gonna be all right, just call me if you need anything. Besides, I'm still working with you. We have counseling to get set up, for these very issues you're feeling right now. A lot of people suffer depression from being separated from their former life. Don't worry, I'm going to help you get through this transition, this is what our ninety days is all about."

They found Daisy's dorm and unlocked the door. A young woman was standing in the middle of the floor looking at a calendar poster she had just hung on the wall.

"Hi, my name is Paige, Paige Hunter." She smiled, extending her hand as Daisy walked in the door.

"Hi, I'm Da..." she quickly caught herself remembering her new name. "Diana, Diana Poitier," she said, extending her hand and taking Paige's into hers.

"I'm Diana's aunt, you can call me Lori," said Lori, though she was obviously a completely different race than Daisy.

Maybe she's an aunt through marriage. Paige smiled as she greeted her new roommate, a little upset that she'd no longer have the space to herself.

Lori Snelling stood quietly as she watched Paige, carefully making a mental note to investigate her and run her through central, make sure she wasn't a risk for Daisy. She stepped outside the room and used a paging device that had a keyboard attached to ask her unit to do a background check on Daisy's roommate. She'd know more about this girl than this girl knew about herself in less than three point six minutes.

"If you need anything just let me know," said Paige, who was already settled, having moved into the dorm back in August when school began. She had the entire wall on her side of the room completely decorated with posters, calendars, and her life's accomplishments. It was a little late for Daisy to have a problem with the left side of the room. Paige had already taken the twin bed and the wall on the right.

"Yeah, sure, it's fine. This side is just great." Daisy smiled, looking at Paige, who was so stunningly beautiful that Daisy couldn't stop looking at her. She had long black hair and big brown eyes. She definitely appeared to be mixed, although Daisy wasn't sure with what, maybe Spanish, maybe Asian, definitely black, but she had no idea of Paige's nationality at first glance.

"Well, I'm hungry, would you like me to bring you back something from the campus market?"

"Oh, no, I'm fine, thanks," said Lori.

"Yeah, I'm fine, too," said Daisy, thinking how lucky she was to have a nice, pretty roommate.

"Okay, well I'll be back, guys," said Paige as she closed the door.

The room was smaller than Daisy had expected, but at least her roommate seemed nice enough. Her bed felt great as she sat down on it, testing the mattress for firmness.

"Not bad, right?" asked Lori.

"No, it's not bad at all."

"Well, I'm going to let you get settled," Lori said, looking around the room, figuring it was best to let Daisy get comfortable in her new surroundings. She hugged Daisy and again promised she was only a phone call away. Daisy watched as she closed the door behind her. She looked around the room. It was hard to believe she was actually there. It was certainly a far cry from the rough inner-city streets of Philadelphia.

Diana Abigail Poitier. She smiled at the thought of her new life and her new name. She spun around in a circle in the middle of the room before falling backward onto her bed. She had many plans for getting her life together. She was lucky to have gotten out of West Philadelphia and lucky to have another chance at life. She planned to do everything in her power to do the right thing and live a good life. At first she had been upset, but not anymore, everything for her would fall into place, her life wouldn't be wasted. She had the power to be anybody in the world she wanted to be and she planned to use it. *I think this might really work out.*

Tommy and Merva drove up Susquehanna Avenue and turned on Twenty-third Street, pulling up in front of 2234 N. Twenty-third Street, where police tape was hanging across the front door of the house, sealing off the home. Not even the family was to enter until forensics removed the tape.

"Let's take a look," said Tommy as they both closed the car doors behind them. Technically, he wasn't supposed to, but, who followed the rules anymore?

Merva carried a camera and began snapping pictures. She walked down the block as Tommy looked around outside and on the porch. There were tire tracks in the street, and Merva took several photos of them, hoping that they would offer some type of evidence later down the line. She took pictures of the bullet-riddled front porch and the bullet-shattered window and then made her way up the porch steps.

"Think we should speak to any of the neighbors? You never know, maybe someone saw something," said Merva, knowing that even if someone did see something, nine times out of ten, they wouldn't be willing to offer any information to the police.

"I saw something," said an old man a few houses down sitting on his porch.

"Really, what's your name, sir?" asked Tommy as he pulled out his pen and pad and walked down the steps over to where the man was sitting on his porch.

"Clarence Wilson," the man said, not caring about the thugs that were terrorizing the neighborhood. He wasn't afraid and would be damned if he would be.

"It was a silver Oldsmobile. It came through here last night just a little after seven o'clock. I was going in the house when I noticed the car moving slower than a turtle, then it got…I'd say…maybe twenty, twenty-five feet from their house and the driver just started firing. I hurried up and got out the way and got in the house and next thing I heard the gunfire stopped and the car took off speeding down the block."

"Were you able to see the driver or the tag number of the vehicle, sir?" asked Merva.

"No, I didn't see the driver. I had to get in the house and get out the way, I told you, but it was a silver Olds, I saw that much," Mr. Clarence said, for sure knowing that much was true.

"Do you know the make, sir, or the year of the car?"

"Well, I think it might have been an Oldsmobile, but I couldn't tell you the year. It wasn't new," added Mr. Clarence, as if that was all he could remember.

"Here you go, sir, here's my card. If you can think of anything at all, please call the number right here," said Tommy, making sure the older gentleman knew how to reach him if he thought of anything else.

"Do you know if Beverly's gonna make it? I saw the paramedics taking her body out the house last night."

"We don't know yet, sir. We're gonna be stopping by the hospital to speak with some of the family members that were inside at the time of the drive-by," said Merva. "We're hoping that maybe one of the family members inside can give us a little assistance in helping catch the perpetrator.

"Oh, okay, that sounds good," said Mr. Clarence.

"If you want call that number on the card, we'll let you know and we'll keep you posted."

"Well thank you so much, I sure do appreciate it," said Mr. Clarence. "I hope you find whoever did this and get 'em off the streets."

"That's what we're here to do," said Tommy as he and Merva walked back to the car.

"Let's pay a visit to Mrs. Robertson's and then stop by Jefferson and check on the victim," said Merva, as if it sounded like a plan.

"And I'll have central search this silver Oldsmobile, see if anything pops up. We might get a lead."

"That's a long shot without the tag," commented Merva.

"Yeah, but you never know," said Tommy.

"Yeah, you never know," said Merva as she walked down the street, checking out the neighborhood.

The two of them cut through the park to West Philadelphia where Mrs. Robertson lived. An SPCA van was parked outside to rescue Boots. The detectives in the homicide unit had called for them to take away her now-homeless pet.

"Hey, kitty, kitty," squeaked Merva.

"You serious?" Tommy asked, as they made their way inside the building and up to the fifth floor where Mrs. Robertson's body had been found in her doorway. A white tape outline showed the exact position of Mrs. Robertson's body, which had just been removed from the crime scene before they got there.

Detectives and police officers combed the older woman's apartment. Tommy walked in, careful not to disturb the crime scene.

"Watch it, Delgado, that's where her cat was sitting," said Detective Monahan.

"It's a doorway, Monahan, I have to walk through like everybody else," answered Delgado, wanting to tell him to take a hike.

"Look at all this blood," Merva said, staring at the floor as if she hadn't seen that much blood in her life.

"Come on, what you waiting for?" asked Tommy, wondering why she was so hesitant.

For Merva, the hardest thing about her job was the crime scenes. It was something that she couldn't get used to no matter how many times she investigated them. The blood, the bodies, and the smell of it left her nauseated and light-headed; it always did. Merva stepped over the puddles of blood in the same footprints as Tommy. She walked past him and into the apartment and looked into the kitchen, then the living room. She had on gloves and a pair of investigating tweezers to pick things up and she was always careful not to disturb anything that might be considered evidence. She knew that there was nothing worse than contaminated evidence.

"What's this?" asked Tommy, still at the door in the hallway, next to the blood, next to where the body was. He picked up a tiny piece of orange tiger lily petal with his tweezers. He held it up to Merva's face.

"I don't know," she said, examining the piece of petal before Tommy placed it in a small bag.

"Well, I'll tell you by dinnertime," said Tommy, lifting his eyebrow as if he were Inspector Gadget.

"Okay, let me know," said Merva. She walked back toward the living room, as Tommy bent back down and scoured the floor for evidence.

"I got something!" shouted Merva, as if she had found a missing link to the universe.

Tommy quickly stood up and moved to stand next to her in the living room. She faced the far right wall, where some pictures were sitting on a shelf next to several basketball trophies, with award plaques hanging neatly on the wall behind them.

"You see what I see?" asked Merva as she read the plaques on the wall, looked at the pictures, and read the endorsements on the trophies.

"Fuck me, I didn't even pay attention to the old man," said Tommy as he read, mumbling to himself. "In recognition of fine sportsmanship, this certifies that Lance Robertson is West Philadelphia High... Oh, shit!"

"Lance Robertson," they said simultaneously as they stared at each other. "Bernard Guess," they said, again simultaneously. "The Somerset murders."

"He was one of the burglars."

"Yeah, him and the Jeremy Tyler guy. They climbed a tree and went through the bathroom window to rob the guys inside," added Merva.

"Fuck, this shit ain't over," said Tommy as he pulled out his book, looking back at his notes. "Oh, shit, Twenty-third and Susquehanna, 2234 N. Twenty-third Street, drive-by, gunshot victim down at Jefferson, guess who?" said Tommy, looking at Merva and trying to figure out why he hadn't put the pieces together long before now.

"Who?"

"Beverly Guess? Bet your ass that's Nard's house, or his family house, and Beverly Guess is a relative, and we're talking payback time, big-time, from the looks of it," Tommy said, looking around.

"Shit, you're right! Why the hell didn't I see it sooner?" she asked the air. "This shit ain't over, Tommy, this case isn't settled."

"Oh, no, it's not over at all, and by the looks of it, we're just getting started."

"Come on, let's get over to the hospital, see if we can speak to the gunshot victim," said Merva, like Deputy Dog, ready for action.

"Ross, her gunshot wound is to the head," said Tommy. "I don't think she's going to be up for questioning today."

"You never know, it's worth a shot."

"Yeah, you never know," said Tommy, stepping over Monahan as he followed her out the door.

North Philly
12:30 p.m.

Dizzy walked in from the outside. He slowly made his way down a hallway, down a flight of stairs, and into the back room of the basement.

"It's colder than Jack Frost's ass," alerted Dizzy as he closed the door behind him. Simon always made him use pay phones outside.

"What happened to the boy?"

"DeSimone came through, the boy made off like a one-eyed leprechaun with a pot of gold." Dizzy smiled as he gave his old-timer cohort five like it was 1973. "He got three to eight years, eligible for parole in about eighteen months. Plus DeSimone said his uncle's friend is head of the parole board, so the kid's out of there in a year and half. You can't beat that with a magic stick."

"What about the kid's mother?"

"Aww, naw, they saying she's not going to make it."

"Damn shame," said Simon, shaking his head. "You know, when we was coming up, wasn't no innocent like it is today, no women, no children. Shit made sense, common sense, and you only did what you had to do to survive. And the fight...shit, the fight was for the power. We fought the system for equality and justice. Shit...we stood up for Martin, but we got down with Malcolm."

"Give me some," said Dizzy, holding his hand out for a soul brother five before Simon continued.

"Shit, today...I don't know, man...I don't know. Seem like all the shit we was fighting for don't mean nothing."

"Only thing mean something is that green. Times are changing, man, its 1986, and 1987 'bout to ring in. Right now, it's every man for their self. Did I tell you I seen Chester?"

"Chester, Chester who?"

"You remember Chester, the nigga so black he look blue," joked Dizzy. "He used to run the numbers for Mimms down the bottom off of Girard Avenue."

"Oh, yeah, whatever happened to him?"

"Man, I saw him the other day out Southwest Philly on Fifty-fourth and Hadfield, man, oh, man, the boy was smoked out of his mind."

"Freebasing?"

"I think he smoking that other shit. What do they call it again?"

"Crack?"

"Yeah, that crack shit everybody running around here like wild banshees with," said Dizzy, as if crack were definitely something different from freebasing. He was sure as sure could be. "He scared the shit out of me, came up from behind me, I turned around, and I swear to God I thought he was about to rob me, until his beady little eyes recognized who I was." Dizzy paused to catch his breath, looking at Simon as if the shit wasn't funny. "Then once this joker realized who he was about to rob"—Simon laughed harder as Dizzy continued—"he asked me for a couple of dollars, said his car was broke down around the corner."

"You give it to him?" asked Simon, cocking his head to look at Dizzy over his Gazelle eyeglass frames. Simon had to see this answer.

"You damn right, I gave it to him, you know...I just wanted to get away from him. The nigga looked scary to me, man, he was high out his fucking mind."

"You, not you, Dizzy." Simon laughed, glad to hear somebody had finally shaken up the big guy. "I know you ain't go in your tight-ass pockets for no god damn Chester."

"You should have seen him. Man, I went in my pocket so fast, I couldn't get that nigga away from me quick enough," Dizzy responded, laughing with his friend.

Simon was quiet for a minute, thinking of Nard, who had stayed true for him and never said his name, and now he was facing time in a Pennsylvania state penitentiary for it. Simon wasn't a fool, prison time was prison time. At least the kid only had a few years to do. Nard was still just a kid, though, just turned twenty-one. Simon knew how the mind worked inside and how rough prison life could be. Everybody was well aware that Simon admired Nard for being the soldier that he was; the boy could have brought him a lot of trouble, a lot of heat. But he didn't. Simon would never forget it. "Where you say they taking him?"

"Prentice said up Graterford," responded Dizzy, still thinking about the ghost of Chester he had bumped into the other day.

"I'll make a few calls over to Graterford, have them on the lookout for him, make sure the boy be all right." Simon had more favors owed to him inside the penitentiary than he did out on the streets, so calling in a favor or two for Nard wouldn't be a problem. "And Chester's on drugs, huh?"

"That ain't no drugs. That crack shit they running in them streets is something else. I don't know; I got a bad feeling."

"What you mean?"

"The people when they high off that shit, it's like they forget," said Dizzy, staring off into space.

"Forget what?"

"Forget they people, man. They not right," he said, still enchanted at his first encounter with a true crackhead. "Listen to me, Simon, that crack shit, that's some other shit for real. Who the fuck would put water on they cocaine? Let alone mix that shit with some baking soda, who could have thought of that? And they cook that shit in test tubes, I heard," said Dizzy, still serving kilos of fish scale. "I'm telling you this shit right here is gonna change the game, in a real bad way."

"Man, come on, can't nothing be worse than heroin, the way these fools need a fix."

"It's different, this crack shit is different. Chester looked like…I don't know, his eyes, I could see right through him, and you know what?"

"What?"

"He didn't have no soul. It was like he was a zombie. He was there but then he wasn't there. Watch, this crack thing, it's gonna be big. Personally, I think it's already some kind of epidemic, just like that show said…umm…what was it, oh yeah, *48 Hours on*

Crack Street. I'm telling you, Simon, this might be the end."

"Be what end?" questioned Simon, as if it couldn't be that serious.

"The end for these niggas out here who smoke that shit."

Temple Hospital
2:30 p.m.

Beverly lay still, her eyes shut, her body limp, as she was still unconscious after having suffered the head injury. It was by God's grace that the bullet had merely grazed the back side of her head. However, the impact was a shock and hit her hard enough to cause a severe concussion. The neurosurgeon couldn't guarantee when she'd wake, and if she did, if she'd be a hundred percent. He claimed nothing except that the surgery to remove the bullet from her shoulder blade had gone well. The rest, according to him, was up to God's mercy, but his part was done. The doctor had performed his job with skill, rushing her into the operating room and draining fluids from her brain and stopping the blood from the wound to the back of her head. Uncle Ray Ray sat next to Beverly watching *The Young and the Restless,* every now and then rubbing her arm and her hand.

Uncle Ray Ray picked up the business card from the side table next to the hospital bed. He looked at the card: Detective Thomas Delgado. He looked at the card again and the number. The detective's extension was 127. *I should play that number,* he thought to himself, wishing there was more information he could have offered them. They seemed real concerned about finding the person who did the drive-by. And they even seemed to believe that they would catch the person or persons responsible. They spent an hour talking to Uncle Ray Ray. He told them everything that happened, how he was on his way into the kitchen to talk with his son Chris when the first bullet pierced the window. He told them how he ducked down on the floor and how his niece was hit. After they spoke with Uncle Ray Ray, they spoke with the attending physician and got an update on Beverly's injuries and prognosis, but he wouldn't know the extent of the injuries until she regained consciousness.

"So that's Bernard Guess's mother and great-uncle," said Merva, putting the family tree together and connecting the dots.

"You thinking what I'm thinking?" asked Tommy.

"I don't know, but if you're thinking what I'm thinking, this case is definitely not over."

"The captain's not going to like this. It's going to keep the Somerset murder case in the news," noted Tommy.

"The captain, try the chief. The last thing he wants, I'm sure, is to even hear the name Somerset, right about now," said Merva, shaking her head.

"Hey, Mr. Guess," said Tyrone, walking through the door.

"Oh, Lord, here comes weasel," mumbled Ray, easing over to an unconscious Beverly. "Wherever did you get this nigga from, I don't know. It really beats the hell out of me," he said, still whispering in her ear.

"I'm sorry; you say something, Mr. Guess?" asked Tyrone, smiling politely.

"Umm…no, I said, I'm glad you visitin', I can get a sandwich and some tea," said Beverly's uncle, just as crazy as always, raising his voice when he said the word "tea."

"What's the doctor's saying? Is she doing better?" asked Tyrone, full of hope.

It was at that moment that Ray actually had a soft spot, a gentle moment, an epiphany of sorts, and he could see Tyrone's love and care for Beverly, clearly see it.

"Naw, son, I'm sorry, the doctor said she's still unconscious. I just been sitting here hoping she'd wake up. The bullet grazed the back of her head, but it didn't do no damage. They took the bullet out her shoulder. The doctor said she might not be able to lift her arm over her head no more and she might have some nerve damage but he won't know that until she wakes up."

"Well, when she gonna do that?" asked Tyrone, wishing Beverly would come on.

"I don't know, son. I don't know," said Uncle Ray as he looked at his niece. "The world is really changing. Back when I was coming up, nothing like this ever happened. Wasn't nobody even thinking of a gun. I wonder where they getting them from?" Uncle Ray asked Tyrone, looking at him.

"I guess they selling them, that's what everybody says. The government sells them and illegal guns end up in our communities."

"I wish they would stop," said Uncle Ray. "I really wish they would stop." Uncle Ray Ray let go of Beverly's hand, having had his fingers intertwined with hers. "I'm going to the cafeteria and get a cup of coffee...I mean tea," said Ray, "You want something while I'm down there?"

"No, thanks, I'm all right, Mr. Guess," he said, taking the seat Ray had occupied next to Beverly. It had been just a few days since the incident. But three weeks later, Beverly's body would remain asleep, as if only a shell was left behind. Couldn't no one be missing her more than Tyrone. With all he had to say, all his fussing, all his harshness, his tongue-lashings at times and his forgetfulness of anything remotely kind, especially on special holidays, birthdays, or any occasion that called for a celebration, there was no one more broken at the sight of Beverly than he.

"What did they do to you, baby? What did they do? They don't know what they did when they took you from me, baby, they don't know what they done took from me." It was all he could say at the sight of Beverly's frail, worn-down body after she came out of surgery, eleven days and counting, and her head was still wrapped up, tubes draining blood from her brain. It knocked Tyrone off his feet, to say the least. He was always harsh, brassy, and extremely vulgar at times. But even as big, egotistical, and cold as he was, the sight of Beverly crashed his world, leaving him broken. He took his hat off, placed her hand in his, and began to rub her fingers as he lay his head gently on the side of the bed next to her body.

"How you feeling, Beverly?" he asked, as if talking to the air. The doctors told everyone that it was good for her if they could talk to her. So he did, every day after work, and then on the weekends when he came to visit. He had been pleading with her, begging her, and even bargaining with her to wake up. He had promised her everything under the sun and then some. All he wanted was for her to just come back. After thirteen years of being with her, he finally realized how special and amazing she was, faced with the possibility of losing her. He had made every promise in the world to himself, to her, and to God, if she'd just wake up. He even promised he wouldn't cheat no more.

"Please, baby, please, come on and wake up. Beverly, it just ain't right no more without you, baby. I promise, I'll be a better to you. I'll be the man you been deservin' all these years, just come on back," he said, tears running down his face, his head still resting on her bed next to her body.

Every day he pleaded with her, tormented at the fact that she hadn't awakened. "See, it just ain't working now. I don't know if I'm coming or going and I miss you so mu—" He stopped short, realizing he had company in the room. "Hey, Rev, hey Maeleen, what ya'll doing here?" asked Tyrone as he jumped up, wiping his face.

"We just came to see how she was doing," answered Rev.

"Yeah, its been three weeks now and she ain't home yet, so we came on down here to fix her on up and get her on out of here. The power of His Holiness can get her walking and talking, in Jesus' name, give sister Beverly your strength and bring her back, say amen," said Maeleen, at the foot of the bed, rubbing Beverly's feet.

"Amen!" shouted Rev, like a cheerleader assigned to her squad.

"Are y'all okay?" asked Tyrone, wondering what in the world was up with Beverly's crazy-ass neighbors.

"Get her two middle fingers, Rev, and tie them together for me, on the left hand first, Rev. Do the left hand first, then the right fingers, okay, and don't forget what I told you, put a little of the oil I gave you to rub on her between her fingers when you put them together," said Maeleen, opening up some folded aluminum foil.

"What's that?" asked Tyrone, a little concerned. He knew Rev, he was Donna's brother, and Maeleen was a neighbor, but Beverly didn't really associate with either of them as far as he could recall. She always said they were crazy and to stay away from them.

"Just something to help get that blood moving in the body," she quickly answered, not answering at all. "Put it in back of her earlobes, Rev, both of them."

"What in the world is that smell? God damn y'all, that shit stinks!"

"Yeah, but we got to heal her up," said Rev, smiling at Maeleen as if he were Mr. Fix-It Man.

"Heal her up? The smell alone should snap her out of it.

Damn, I can't breathe," Tyrone said, his nostrils unable to bear the stench in the air from whatever Maeleen had had wrapped in the aluminum foil.

"Here, give me a match," said Maeleen, her back now to Tyrone.

"A match? Watchoo doing needs fire? I don't know about lighting no fires in here, what about the oxygen and all the tubes?" Tyrone asked, worried they were going to harm Beverly, or worse, blow the whole building up.

"Nothing, we just lighting candles, that's all."

Candles? thought Tyrone. *What the hell is they into?*

"Go on, baby, take him on out of here," said Maeleen, tired of him irritating her with his ninety-nine questions and unnecessary concern.

"Come on, Tyrone, come on with me we'll go get some coffee," said Rev, putting his arm around his neighbor's shoulder.

"I can't leave her side," he said, pulling away from Rev.

"Yes you can, go on, so I can pray, I don't want nobody in here while I'm praying," snapped Maeleen in a tone that commanded Tyrone to do as he was being told.

"Okay," said Tyrone, hearing only her concern for what she was trying to do. "I do need a cup of coffee," he said, following Rev out of the door like a robot, unable to remember what he was about to say.

The two walked down the hall to the coffee machine located in the waiting area on the floor. They got two cups of coffee and walked back up the hall.

"You go on and have a seat. I'll check on Beverly."

Rev went into the room while Tyrone sat outside the door. In less than two minutes Uncle Ray Ray walked up to him and stood over him.

"What you doing out here?" he asked, startling Tyrone, who honestly hadn't heard him.

"Rev and Maeleen came and Maeleen said she wanted to pray for her, and I went and go..." Tyrone didn't need to say more. Uncle Ray Ray headed for the door to Beverly's room while Tyrone was still speaking.

"What, what's wrong?" asked Tyrone as Uncle Ray Ray opened the door to Beverly's room, interrupting Maeleen's séance with lighted candles and a stench in the air that would turn a skunk running the other way. Maeleen had her arms stretched above her head and was standing over Beverly, chanting, or praying, as she called it.

Any other given Sunday, as if he were Jamie himself, he would have whooped and hollered, but not today. His niece's prognosis wasn't for the better, it was for the worse. So what harm could Maeleen do. *Awww, never mind, no way.* He closed the door behind him as Maeleen snapped her fingers at him and shooed him out of the room.

Crystal and the baby showed up at the hospital just as Uncle Ray Ray was sitting back down.

"You don't want to go in there right now," advised Ray. "She's a little busy," he noted sarcastically and nodded at Rev.

"Yeah, it won't be much longer, trust me, Beverly gonna be up and walking and talking and everybody's gonna call it a miracle. But the power of the Holy Ghost is strong," he said, nodding. "Real strong," he agreed with himself.

Lord have mercy, this boy is crazy, somebody really needs to get him some help. Uncle Ray Ray just looked Rev up and down, wishing all the best for his poor soul.

Crystal and the baby took a seat next to Ray Ray. She told him how she and her momma had made up and her momma wanted her to move back home. Ray was silent for a moment, not saying a word.

"If you ever need to come back, you and the baby, you just come on back home, you understand?"

Thank you, Uncle Ray Ray, you're the best uncle I ain't never have," she said, smiling.

"You just remember what I said, you and that baby always got a place to stay with me and Beverly," he said, thinking to himself how that would have sounded if he had to say it without Beverly on the end. He had lived with Beverly and Nard for the past twelve years. Now, Crystal and the baby were going back home with her momma and he would be going home to an empty house tonight.

"Thanks, Uncle Ray Ray," she said, giving him a hug.

"I'm gonna miss you, little girl," he said, patting the baby on her head. "You woke me up every night, but that's okay. I'm still gonna miss you."

It was a tearful good-bye for Ray Ray and Crystal. Even Tyrone and Rev were wiping their eyes when Ray Ray happened to glance at them.

"Rev, what the hell is wrong with you?"

"I can't take it, it's just so sad."

"Boy, be quiet and go check on Maeleen, make sure she don't got Beverly in that motherfucker floating up to the ceiling or worse."

"Worse how?" asked Tyrone nervously.

"God only knows, son, God only knows."

Green Prison, Waynesburg, Pennsylvania
6:30 p.m.

As darkness fell upon the city of brotherly love, Nard sat lonely in a tiny four-by-six cell in the isolation unit. He had been transported by bus from CFCF up on State Road, where he had stayed for the past six months waiting for trial. He had gotten comfortable at CFCF, accustomed to the routine. However, he was whisked away and deported to Green, a state penitentiary located in Waynesburg, Pennsylvania. Upon arrival, he and a group of seven others were subjected to intake. He was sprayed for bugs, lice, crabs, and any other type of growing infestation one could think of. His hair was cut to meet the prison intake standards, no afros, no braids, no dreads, no hair. But, once in population, he could grow his hair like a beanstalk to the sky if he wanted. For the next two weeks he would sit in a cell, no mail, no phone calls, no human contact, no nothing. It was standard intake for all new inmates to go through isolation. Afterward, he would be brought into the prison population, assigned a block, and assigned to a cell where Wink already had his people waiting for him to touch down.

He lay on his metal bunk connected to the cylinder wall. The reality that he wasn't going home began to set in. He thought about the holidays, Thanksgiving, Christmas, and the New Year that was approaching. He wouldn't have the holidays with his mom, and Uncle Ray Ray, and his cousins. He thought of Chris, and wondered if the family knew he was strung out on drugs. He knew because he had been selling drugs to him. He missed his family life, his mother and Uncle Ray Ray. He thought of his mother, silently, and deep down inside he knew that the drive-by hadn't been accidental. *Please God, please don't let her die.* He had begged his counselor to let him visit her. But he had already been found guilty and wasn't being released, he was in holding waiting for sentencing, he never had bail when he was waiting for trial, he sat all that time. The only good thing was that he'd get those six months back for time served. After the prison denied him the opportunity to visit his mother, he realized how much colder life would seem without her, not that it wasn't cold enough, but without his mother, it would be freezing.

Please don't let my mother die, God. Please don't let her die. He bargained with God, pleading for his mother's life, not even thinking of his own. Little did he know, he would be the one needing all the prayers he could get. He rolled over, facing the cold, hard cinderblock wall. *I wish I was home, please God get me out of here.*

Later That Night
1:16 a.m.

It was the middle of the night. The phone was ringing like an alarm. Tommy rolled over, looked at the green numbers on his clock radio. *It's one-sixteen, who the fuck is calling me in the middle of the night?* He answered the call on the third ring as Vivian rolled away from him.

"Who is it?" she mumbled.

"It's okay, go back to sleep," he said, brushing her hair out of her face.

"What the fuck is wrong? It's the fucking middle of the night."

"Meet me outside."

The line went dead. Tommy cradled the handset and lay it back down on the receiver.

He picked up his pants, slid on a pair of Converse sneakers, and grabbed a jacket. He looked at Vivian. She was knocked out, sleeping like a baby.

He made his way outside. Walked down the street to the corner and spotted a triple black 1986 Cadillac Seville with the slanted back parked down the street. He got into the car as Patricio started the engine.

"Where we going?" asked Tommy, wondering where Patricio was taking him.

"Fucking cops keep riding by me, looking at me like they ain't got shit else to do. What the fuck is wrong with your fucking people?" he asked his cousin, slapping his shoulder as he laughed at him.

"What the fuck is wrong with you? It's the middle of the night."

"Eh, come on, we ain't going far."

Patricio took a quick ten-minute ride to an old steel factory. He drove through the security station and to the back of a building. He parked the Cadillac next to two other Cadillacs.

"Come on, we caught that fucking mole Internal Affairs had tracking you."

"No fucking way, that fast, how'd you know?"

"You know how it is, Tommy. It's as simple as picking up a pay phone and as quick as a payoff," he joked, slamming his car door. "Come on, let's go."

They walked into the building. The sounds of torture and a woman screaming could be heard the moment they walked through the door.

"What the fuck, it's a woman?"

"Hey, pain is all we got, Tommy. This bitch was investigating you, trying to take us out. You hear me? The family...only God knows. I'm telling you, it could have been really bad for the family, Tommy, really bad for the family."

Patricio swung the door open and held it open for Tommy. Tommy walked into the room, his eyes bulging out of his head.

"Merva?" he looked twice, unable to believe she was the rat that his family had caught. "Merva Ross, she's Internal Affairs?"

he asked his cousin. "You got to be kidding me," he joked to his cousin, until he heard Merva speak.

"Tommy, please, Tommy, please, I won't say a word, Tommy, please. I won't say a word. I swear on everything, Tommy, please help me, Tommy."

Tommy looked at Merva. Her wrists were tied tightly and her body was dangling from a metal hook above her head. She was bleeding from her mouth, her makeup worn and stained from crying.

"What the fuck?" He spun around and began pacing. He pulled out a pack of Marlboro Lights from his back pocket, turned, and faced her.

"Why would you even take the case from Internal Affairs in the first place? Why didn't you come and tell me?" he yelled at her. "Why?" he said, grabbing the side of her face, really not wanting to have to hurt her.

"Please, Tommy, I'm sorry. I had no choice, Tommy, they made me report to them... I didn't know what to do."

"Report, what? What did you tell them?" he asked, demanding an answer with the tone of his voice as he squeezed the sides of her head, shaking it in the palms of his hands.

She hesitated as if she didn't know what to say.

"What the fuck did you tell them?" he yelled at her again.

"Tommy, fuck this nigger pig, she'll fucking answer me when I'm fucking done. I'll know everything she told them," Joey said, holding up a pair of jumper cables as he watched Frankie tear off a piece of electrical tape from the roll to cover Merva's mouth. Joey checked the jumper cables, making sure they were securely connected to an electrical unit that would supply doses of electrical shocks to Merva once the cable touched her skin. Joey turned the electricity on and indicated the cables he was holding with his eyes. Frankie moved slowly toward her, placing the electrical tape over her mouth, no longer giving her any options. Her eyes pleaded with Tommy to save her life.

"Fuck, man! Merva, what the fuck is wrong with you!" He couldn't believe it was her. He couldn't believe she was the one investigating him for Internal Affairs. "Why you!" he screamed at her. "Why?" he asked as he spun around, thoughts flashing in and out of his mind. He stopped, focused, pointed to his cousin Joey and his cousin Frankie.

"Find out everything she knows."

He turned and walked out of the room, unable to watch as they would indeed torture her half to death. Pain had a way of making people talk no matter how strong the will. Two cigarettes and ten minutes later Patricio emerged from the building holding Merva's pinky toe in one hand and a pair of cutting shears in the other.

"What the fuck?" asked Tommy, looking at his cousin, covered in burgundy blood.

"I only cut off her pinky toe," he responded, looking just like the cat who ate the canary. "I don't think they know too much. She knows you are a Gatto, though, so you're definitely not hiding behind that corny name of yours in the department."

"The department knows my real name?"

"Yeah, and they know that we are an organized crime family. But she doesn't know much more than that. She said they came to her last year to investigate any possible dealings with you and your organized crime family. She said her report on you was clean. She swears on everything she reported no activity in organized crime of any sort on your part and she said it was submitted over a month ago."

Tommy looked up into the sky, then down at the ground, then at Patricio.

"But umm... I just wanted to make sure you want us to kill her, right?"

"I just can't believe it's Merva."

"Why? Why can't you believe this bitch is a fucking rat?"

"I'm with her every day. I never had a clue."

"Well, stop fucking partying at night, drinking and doing drugs, going to work high, and pay attention, Tommy. You're a fucking cop, come on, for Pete's sake, whadda you expect?"

"No, really, I was with her every day. She was my partner."

"Well, good for her, she had you fooled, so all that makes her is a clever rat, but a rat is still a rat, and they can't be trusted, Tommy. Tell me what to do."

"We kill Ross, they're just going to send someone else," said Tommy, thinking out loud.

"And we'll pinpoint the next one, Tommy, just like we always do. It's what we do, we catch rats and we exterminate them, we're the mob," nodded Patricio, his smile devious.

"You're right, you're always right, Patricio."

"Frankie wants to cut off her head, you don't mind, do you?" asked Patricio in solemn sincerity. "I mean..." he said, throwing his hands in the air, waving the cutting shears and Merva's toe around, "being as though she was your partner and all, I just want to make sure you don't have no problems or nothing with that?" he questioned his cousin, making sure that Tommy knew they were going to dismember her, ripping her body apart; every limb, every finger, every toe.

"Frankie can do whatever he wants, just so long as they never find her body, Patricio," he said, kicking a pebble on the ground.

"No problem, Tommy, that's no problem at all. They'll never

find this bitch, you hear me, they'll never fucking find this toe," he said, holding it up in the air, "let alone her fucking body, so don't you worry, okay? I'll make sure Frankie does a real good job in there. Trust me, I'll take care of everything." He turned from his cousin, somewhat troubled. "Tommy, you know Frankie and Joey…I think this shit gets them fucking high. Me…I can't do body parts anymore," he said, twirling Merva Ross's pinky toe between his fingers as he moved his hand, using the toe to express himself. "You know, the blood…it freaks me out later. I have nightmares and everything."

"Really?"

"Fucking A, I'm in therapy from this shit, you know?" Patricio nodded, proud of the fact he was getting help. "Fucking cutting off this bitch's toe has really set me back, though. Maybe I shouldn't have done it," he added, twirling the brown pinky toe between his fingers, thinking seriously of all the money wasted with Dr. Fredericks, his current psychiatrist.

Tommy looked at his cousin. "I believe you."

"You mind if I stay out here with you for a while?"

"Of course not, be my guest."

And he did. Patricio, Frankie, and Joey were silent hit men for the Gatto crime family. They had killed many. And they made their enemies disappear, literally, never to be heard of or found again. They had all kinds of ways of making someone simply vanish. However, somebody like Ross, a police detective, had to be completely disposed of. There was no doubt there would be a manhunt for her once it was determined that she was missing. Thank God, Frankie's younger brother was a zookeeper. They could be at the zoo later, feeding pieces of Merva to the lions and tigers, if they wanted. Frankie's brother could mix her right in with the daily feed. And Carmen's brother, Dave Pangione, who owned and operated a funeral home, could cremate a body, no questions asked. And then there was Patricio's father, who had the concrete trucking company. Merva could be a solid concrete brick in the bottom of the Schuylkill before the sun came up. Or she could be ashes by breakfast, waiting to be scattered in the wind. It was just that easy for them to kill someone and dispose of the body, and everybody knows if there's no body, there's no case, and all Merva Ross would ever be was a missing persons report. Of course, Tommy would have to help hold vigils, and lead the missing persons investigation, which of course he would. He'd even shed a few tears, fearful that she had been abducted, never to be heard of or seen again. And no one would question it, because he was an officer of the law.

DIE AT THE DOOR

The Next Morning
6:21 a.m.

Liddles had followed Wink Tyler for the past two weeks and watched his mother's house every night, every morning, sometimes all day and knew the comings and the goings of the Tyler family like they were his own. Every morning Wink would pick his mother up and give her a ride to work at six-thirty in the morning. Wink would come from either of two locations, his apartment or the spot where he hustled. It was fortunate that this morning was like no other and no one had left the house; all were inside.

He watched the movement of the street carefully. It was a little after six in the morning. He grabbed his vase of tiger lilies and closed his car door, locking it behind him. He made his way up the front porch, pulled the screen door, and knocked, waiting for an answer.

"Who?" shouted a girl's voice behind the door.

"FTD flower delivery for Ms. Tyler," said Liddles as Leslee

head and looked at Liddles with nothing but vengeance, a wrath between the two they could settle in other space at another time. Staring at the Grim Reaper dead on, his eyes asked the same question, "Why?" but he couldn't speak. Liddles shot him in the chest, piercing his heart, finally dropping him. He looked behind him for a split second, and for whatever reason, he felt good; his brother could now rest knowing that he didn't die alone and he didn't die for nothing.

Leslee lay quiet and still, her eyes closed. She pretended to be dead, her mind in prayer, begging God for her life, that she not die, that she was not ready. The last and only one in her house alive, she heard Liddles pick up his oversized bouquet of flowers, and with a handkerchief he had in his pocket, wipe the doorknob before he closed the door behind him, careful not to leave any fingerprints behind him at the crime scene. Within a matter of minutes, Leslee would take her last breath as Liddles walked down the street, using the flowers to shield his face. He got into his car and drove down the block, completely unnoticed. The time was six-twenty-five and the sun was slowly rising over the city, bringing with it a new dawn and a new day.

Vivian rolled over, reaching for Tommy, but he wasn't there. She opened her eyes and looked at the digital clock on the nightstand. It was six-twenty-five in the morning.

"Tommy," she called out, asking if he was there.

"Yeah, honey," she heard him reply from the living room.

Comfortable knowing that he was there, she rolled back over, stretching like a cat before getting out the bed. She went into the bathroom, emerged down the hall and found Tommy, lying on the couch, one hand on his boxers, his other hand dangling off the sofa, a blanket half covering him.

"Why are you out here on the couch?" she asked, as he realized she definitely didn't know he had been out last night.

"I couldn't sleep, babe. I was just tossing and turning all night. I came out here so I wouldn't wake you," he lied, holding her body close to him.

"You want some coffee?"

"I think we should get married, Vivian; let's go down to City Hall, you want?" he asked, with more motives than a serial killer.

"Tommy, are you all right, you got a fever or something, 'cause I know you're joking, right?" Vivian asked, sounding more and more Italian every day.

"Would I kid around about something like this?" he asked.

"Oh, my God, I love you," she exclaimed. "I love you, Tommy, I swear you're the best!"

"Good morning, kiddo, it's a beautiful, bright, and sunny morning." Nurse Hanzer pulled back the curtains and let the sun shine in as she did every morning. Faithfully, she serviced her patients as if they actually would respond to her. She worked the coma ward and the ICU station of the hospital where Beverly was so that she could be properly monitored. Because she wasn't awake, she needed special care, special monitoring, and Nurse Hanzer took care of her patients as if they were indeed her very own children. The best part about her job was that she had no patients to trouble her. No one wanted ice, chips, water, Jell-O, juice, help to the bathroom, an extra blanket, a bed change, or a bath, or needed a question answered, because all of them were sleeping like little angels.

Walking into room 1624, she never once realized Beverly was fully awake, lying in her bed, eyes open, staring straight at her. Beverly could hear Nurse Hanzer moving about the room, speaking to her, the sudden bright light blinding her as Nurse Hanzer threw back the curtains. She closed her eyes, opened them again, and let her pupils dilate. Nurse Hanzer was standing above her, reading the monitors and writing down Beverly's stats.

"Wow, you're doing great, kiddo," she said, still not aware that Beverly was watching her every move. "It's six-thirty-seven, sleepyhead, time you woke up and got your morning cup of coffee…Oh, my Lord and savior, somebody help," she screamed, dropping her chart as her eyes met Beverly's and she realized her patient was conscious.

She immediately ran out the room as if she had just seen a ghost. She called out for Nurse Jenkins as she ran over to her station and called into the doctor's unit for immediate assistance. Nurse Jenkins was right behind her as they both ran back into the room within ten seconds, straight to Beverly's bedside. She smiled down on Beverly, rubbing her head and taking her pulse at the same time.

"Oh, my, can you hear me, honey?" asked Nurse Hanzer, as Beverly moved her head up and down, answering yes.

"It's like a miracle," she whispered under her breath to Nurse Jenkins. "Truly a miracle."

1988

COLLEGE LIFE

Arizona State, 1988

"Go, Tigers! YEAHHH!" screamed Daisy. She was cheerleading, "Give me a T, give me an I," as the quarterback threw a perfect pass to Dustin Webb, a wide receiver, who ran the ball from the twenty yard line down the field to score a touchdown to win the game with only three minutes left in the last quarter. The cheerleaders shook their pompoms while screaming to the top of their lungs as they jumped up and down. The Tigers won the game 21–17.

College football was just as exciting as watching pro football on Sunday night. And afterward everyone would gather at McClintock Hall to celebrate. Of course, there'd be several frat parties on campus, too. Daisy wouldn't be able to attend, she had a test the next day in her Physics 101 class. Her grades would never get her on the Dean's List, but they would get her a college diploma. Besides cheerleading, she was pledged to the Alpha Kappa Alpha sorority, worked in the administrative office, and had settled into college life, quite perfectly. She still had plenty of money tucked away. So she was rather well off, with close to fifty thousand dollars, compared to the average college student, who was flat broke and calling home every month for an allowance to get by.

"Hey, Diana, coming to Sean's party?" asked Sandra Boggs as she breezed by on her way to one, if not crashing a few, of the many campus parties.

"No, I'm in the library, probably all night. I got exams in Mr. Deutchel's Physics 101 class tomorrow."

"Oh, no, he's really tough. Good luck." Sandra smiled as she walked past Daisy.

I'ma need it, Daisy thought to herself. She hurried along to study in the campus library, finding it rather empty. After getting settled, she pulled out her study sheet and began her search for a collection of books she would need as study tools. Bending down and filing through a shelf, she accidently backed up, bumping her butt into Webster Praeliou, another student, pushing him into the bookcase shelving.

"Ooops, I'm so sorry," she said, smiling and giggling as she turned around, not realizing that she had knocked his glasses off.

"Oh...um...me, too," said a tall brown-skinned guy, who actually hovered above her at six feet one inches tall.

"Wow, you sure are tall," she said, mistaking him for a basketball player.

"Yeah...," he said locking in on her greenish hazel eyes, unable to stop staring at her. "You sure are beautiful," he remarked, staring at the most beautiful girl he had ever laid his eyes on.

"Awww, thank you," she purred, smiling, batting her eyelashes, and sticking her chest out toward him just a little as she corrected her posture like Mrs. Isaacs had taught her.

"Chest out, shoulders back, head straight, and don't let those books fall off your heads, ladies, let's go, march in your circle, as I have taught you."

She could hear Mrs. Isaacs, her etiquette teacher, in her head, and all the golden rules for being in the presence of a man. "Least is always best when dealing with a man."

That woman was so right. She had taught Daisy so much. It wasn't until Daisy found virtue that she truly understood how ill-mannered she had been in the past and learned how to conduct herself.

"What's your name," he calmly asked, hoping she couldn't sense how nervous he was.

"Diana Poitier," she said, smiling enchantingly at him. "What's yours," she asked right back, showing interest.

"Webster... Webster Praeliou," he said, extending his hand to formalize their introduction.

"It's a pleasure to meet you, Webster," Daisy said as he held her hand in his.

"No, really, the pleasure is all mine."

Daisy talked to Webster at the table where she was supposed to be studying for Mr. Deutchel's final exam all night. The two talked about everything under the sun. It turned out that Webster wasn't a basketball player, he was a doctor, a neurosurgeon, about to begin his residency.

"Wow, that's amazing. I don't think I've ever met anyone as smart as you in my life," she joked, giving him one of many compliments. Daisy was taken with him and his various accomplishments. He was the only man she had ever met who was studying to be a doctor, and the best part was, he was black. And while he was older than she was, his life had been spent studying year after year, making many a social sacrifice to attain his doctorate. Yet the sacrifice for Webster wasn't a burden. It was the challenge placed before him to become the world's top neurosurgeon. It was all part of the Praeliou design sculpted by his father, Webster Praeliou III. His brother, Seth Praeliou, had already won a seat as city councilman at large and was a contender to be the first black senator for the state of Arizona. And one day, part of the design would be for him to run for the presidency. The Praeliou family had been born into vast wealth, stemming from their great-great-grandmother, who was born in New Orleans to a Frenchman and a Creole. She inherited two châteaus in France from her daddy's side and a vast swampland from her momma's great-grandfather, left to her great-grandmother when he died a sudden death of a heart attack. His family was led to the Dotterhouse, expecting a boardinghouse, only to find he had died in a whorehouse. The whore, whoever she was, surely gave him the time of his life, to say the least.

By daybreak, Daisy and Webster were still engulfed in their conversation. And even though both had classes in a couple of hours, they took the last bit of free time they had, and instead of returning to their rooms to freshen for the day, they ended at the coffee shop, sipping coffee, laughing, talking, and falling completely in love with one another. It was indeed a classic storybook romance that blossomed in the library that cold December evening and Daisy had finally found her Prince Charming. Webster was a very caring and a very kind man. Not harsh, not egotistical, and more scientist than ladies' man, all characteristics she was far from accustomed to.

As time passed, Webster would enter his residency. And Daisy would graduate from college in 1990 and quickly use her bachelor's degree in psychology to obtain an entry-level position as a social worker at the Children's Hospital in Phoenix. Up until she met Webster, she had really never experienced a true and honest relationship. Webster made her see her life much more clearly. He was a good-hearted person, a kind soul, and a gentle spirit. He opened doors for her, took her to the best restaurants in and outside of Phoenix and Scottsdale, spent all his free time with her, and called her at least twice a day regardless of how busy he was, just to make sure she was okay. He often offered to buy her things, but Daisy decided that he was too nice and she couldn't take his money. Well, actually, she didn't need it. She had plenty of money still tucked away, thanks to weasel-ass Reggie's trying to be so slick. She actually didn't feel so bad cashing in on her dead momma's Social Security checks after she realized that her account's being frozen was the only thing that had saved her from Reggie getting away with his check scam on her. She thought about all the creeps she had slept with, some of them so deviant that the law had sex codes to arrest such people. Unfortunately, in Daisy's previous line of work, the more deviant they were, the better customers they would become. They could pay, do all sorts of things the average woman would never allow to be done to her body, and leave in a three-piece suit as if leaving a business meeting on Wall Street. Even she was completely humiliated at some of the things she had done for money.

She thought of Webster. The last thing on his mind was fun. He studied the complexities of the brain. The thought of his being able to save people's lives really attracted her to him. He was a fascinating man. Webster lived off-campus and had his own apartment. He cooked, cleaned, and was incredibly neat. His conversation was different, because he didn't speak with the slang she was accustomed to hearing from the guys that she normally dated. His clothes weren't trendy at all, but that was irrelevant. Over time, Daisy came to appreciate Webster more than anyone she had ever met in her life. He became the only person in the world she could truly call her friend. They did everything together, at least everything humanly possible, considering they both had classes.

"Hey, Diana, we're going to the movies. Want to come?" asked Paige, swinging open their dorm room door. She looked like a little girl, with two ponytails on the sides of her head, legging stockings, sheer white pantyhose, a skirt, and a leather jacket, a complete remake of *Pretty in Pink* gone punk rocker. Paige had turned out to be the best friend she ever had, the sister she always wanted, the only person in the world she ever thought of telling the truth to but didn't. She always remembered what Lori Snelling told her.

"Never, ever tell anyone, ever, that you are in police protective custody, or everything you've done, everything we've done getting you here, will be jeopardized, and trust me, no one keeps secrets, someone always tells someone else. Keep this to yourself until the day you die."

Lori held Daisy's shoulders, staring into her eyes, making her promise.

"I won't tell a soul," said Daisy, and she never ever would. That would be one secret she would carry to her grave, and as far as she was concerned Daisy Mae Fothergill never existed.

Whenever anyone asked, she simply made up a story, a good, heartbreaking, tear-jerker story, and people believed her.

"My parents died in a fatal car accident when I was a little girl. My dad's brother and his wife, my aunt Lori, raised me. They're okay, but it's not the same, you know," said Daisy as she pretended to be sad. She would over the years repeat that story until she knew it like the back of her hand and no one would ever think different, especially her roommate, Paige.

"Well, I'm not leaving you here alone for the holidays," said

Paige, now sitting straight and determined. And she did take her home, every year, on every holiday since they had become roommates. Paige opened her heart and her family's home so her friend wouldn't be alone.

"No, I can't go to the movies, I'm going over to Webster's, but maybe next time," said Diana Poitier, who had groomed herself into the perfect college student, with the perfect grades, the perfect friends, and the perfect boyfriend, who would one day be her perfect husband, and she would live a perfect life. It was destined for her.

Green Penitentiary, Waynesburg, Pennsylvania

Nard was only twenty-one when he went inside, a baby. And when you're as young as Nard, with as much notoriety as the Somerset murder case had brought, you're going to have a lot of guys waiting to see just what you're made of when you get there. And that was certainly the case for Nard. But Nard had bigger fish to fry; Nard had a hit put out on him before he even touched down inside Green, and worse, he had no one to hold him down. Wink had already put the word in and Nard was nothing more than a dead man walking.

In prison, it was another world, survival techniques were different, cooking techniques were different, communicating techniques were different, and the art of war was different. There were no guns in prison. You had to man up, and most problems were settled the old-fashioned way, though some were not. Incidents of gang-related violence in Green were commonplace. The warden turned a deaf ear and a blind eye and so did the correctional officers. Anything could happen to you in prison and no one would see a thing and no one would say a word. Your beef was yours to settle and it was every inmate for himself. That's why the gangs were so relevant and very much needed. Who was going to look out for you? If you didn't join a gang, then you joined Islam, and even then there weren't any guarantees that nothing would happen to you.

Life inside Green changed many a man into an animal and many an animal into a beast. Reform and rehabilitation was the pretense created by the prison system to justify itself but the truth was that nobody was getting rehabilitated—if anything, they came home worse than when they went in. And Nard unfortunately was now a number, and for Nard, the road inside Green would be the roughest road of his life.

He remembered the day after he was sentenced and the news that his momma had been shot in the head and was in the hospital, how, behind bars, he couldn't do anything to help her. How he wished his life had turned out differently. Shortly afterward, he was shipped off to Green, his possessions and things from his cell at CFCF packed up and shipped to Green for him. After two weeks of being confined to quarantine he was let out into population. Assigned to D block, cell 14, he clearly had no options but the top bunk. His celly, some nigga from Southwest Philly named Otis, who had a life sentence for a double homicide, would become Nard's worst nightmare. He had it all figured out that Nard would pay his dues to him. Unfortunately, it wasn't just the prison system that did its own special processing while holding an inmate before allowing them to enter population; some of the inmates had their ways of figuring out who was who before ever meeting them. And unfortunately for Nard, Simon Shuller's phone call went to Graterford and not Green. It could have happened to anyone, but Nard had nothing to bargain and no one bargaining for him. Possibly, maybe there was something that could have changed fate, but there wasn't. Inside nobody cared about who you thought you were or what you thought you were doing on the streets. The inside was designed to break you completely down and then build you back up, and very few survived without selling their souls to something or someone.

Nard learned this in less than a month of being in population. He had come inside from the yard, showered, and was back in his cell. Otis smiled kindly, but truth was Otis was nothing but trouble, and usually when people saw him and his crew coming, they went the other way. No one wanted to be a part of trouble. Trouble in prison meant more time. And Otis was notorious for bringing trouble. Otis walked out of the cell without saying a word, but right after he walked out, three men walked in. Set up by his cellmate, Nard tried his best to fight them off. Maybe had the correctional officer assigned to the block called for help or even blown his whistle, maybe just maybe it could have saved Nard. Nard didn't get in one blow before having the wind knocked out of him with an uppercut to his midsection. Nard fell to the floor, unable to breathe.

"We're gonna see just what you're made of, bitch!" His assailant laughed, bending down and picking Nard up.

The air had been knocked out of him, and all he could do was hold his stomach, gasping as he felt his pants being ripped below his knees. Before he could protest, he felt a long, hard dick penetrating him. He tried to free himself, but was sucker punched in the face.

"Take it, nigga," said a big, tall guy everyone called Smitty. Smitty, Mel, and Hawk, all under the orders of Otis, tore into Nard as he tried to fight them off. Overpowered, he continued to struggle. Not once did he give in, fighting as best he could as everyone on the block made it their business to get busy and as far away from what was transpiring as possible. No one would see or hear anything. And if asked, they would all have the same response. "I don't know nothing."

The correctional officer assigned to the block was finishing up a crossword puzzle before making his rounds. Someone shouted out, "Five O!" to alert the others on the block, but more important, Smitty and Hawk.

Smitty dropped the hold he had on Nard's hips, letting his ass go at the same time. He pulled his dick out of Nard and watched Nard fall to the floor in excruciating pain while blood and semen dripped down his legs.

"I'll be back to finish your bitch ass off, ya heard," he said, intending to kill Nard as instructed, but not having enough time because Five O was en route.

"Don't you have something you should be doing?" asked C. O. Parks.

"You right, I do," said Wilson Gray, watching as Smitty, Mel, and Hawk walked back down the block to their own cells, acting as if nothing had happened, and if it did, they didn't know anything about it.

"Break it up and get back to where you belong."

Otis lay down on his bottom bunk and picked up a magazine, acting as if nothing was going on.

When C. O. Parks walked down the hall and looked into the cell, he saw Nard, who was still on the floor, unable to get up, unable to move.

"What the fuck, Otis? What the fuck did you do to him?"

"Man, I ain't did nothing to him. I was out there with you. I just walked back in here and he was laid out on the floor. I don't know what you talking about."

Nard would spend the next week healing in the prison's infirmary. But, as soon as he was sent back to D block, cell 14, it seemed as if Otis and his crew had been doing nothing more than sitting around waiting for his return. Walking down the block, Nard could feel all eyes on him like praying mantises waiting to engulf their prey. The entire block was now ready to take a shot at Nard, and he knew it. Even bitch-ass niggas thought they could try him. It was only a matter of time before they did. And time was something he just didn't have. Little did he know that all that had transpired was because of Jeremy Tyler, a thief, who thought he could rob Nard, and had snuck through a window and gotten his brains blown out. All this was over his dumb ass and a phone call that his dumb-ass brother had made, attempting revenge. Little did Nard know, but he would soon find out.

Merlin Watkins was two cells down. He had silently listened to the attack on Nard from his cell. Merlin understood how Nard was feeling, he, too, had been raped by Otis and his crew. So, he understood how Nard had to be feeling—ashamed, scared, and lonely. Merlin waited and waited, watching the movements of the block. Everybody would be called to go outside, and even though it was freezing cold, the chance for fresh air and walking outside the concrete jungle they lived in had a way of making a nigga feel free, even if there were twelve foot fences and barbed wire surrounding them. When Merlin found a safe zone to move, he walked into Nard's cell, slid one of his handmade wooden knives under Nards pillow, smiled at him, then walked back out the cell, not saying a word.

That's how his sentence started, fucked up, but it wouldn't be how his sentence ended.

North Philadelphia
Beverly's House

Uncle Ray Ray sat quietly, listening to Beverly as she spoke to Mr. DeSimone about Nard and what had happened to him. He had a hundred and one questions to bombard his niece with once she hung up the phone. He looked at Beverly, remembering how it seemed like yesterday that she was lying lifeless in the hospital. Not a day would pass that he didn't thank God for sparing their lives that night. The city murder rate was sky-high, shootouts and drive-bys happened in the inner city every day. Ray didn't understand what was happening to his neighborhood. It just wasn't how he had come up. He was forty-eight years old, and he came up in the sixties and the seventies. There were drugs, always an element of crime, and even gangs, but the fight was for the power, the fight was against the man. And there was a level of solidarity that seemed to be missing among the young men he encountered now.

"I can't believe him, we did everything to get him off, and he beat that case! You mean to tell me he done went to jail and is facing another twenty-five years to life in prison for murder?"

Beverly wanted to throw the phone, but she didn't, she stood still, barely maintaining her composure as tears began to melt down the side of her face.

"Well, what did the lawyer say?"

"He said Nard has been charged with murder. He killed a man, knocked some other guy's eyeball out and squished it in his hand, attacked another guy, stabbing him with a wooden shank and whatever else you can think of," said Beverly, spinning around and falling into the chair next to the phone.

"Did they have the hearing, yet?"

"He said he's going inside now." Beverly shook her head, then put her head in her hands, resting her elbows on her knees. "What's wrong with him?" She looked up at her uncle with tears in her eyes. "He had eighteen months, with his served time, a year if that, and would have been eligible for parole. Why couldn't he just do the years and come home?" Beverly asked, not understanding why her son was spending his life behind bars like some caged animal. She could see him doing the year and then making parole. She had swallowed the pain two years ago when he was first arrested. But now DeSimone was saying he could possibly be sentenced to another fifteen to twenty-five years for a prison murder.

"He told me that he didn't have no choice, Beverly. That could only mean one thing...and if the boy's in there fighting for his life, then he's doing what he got to do to survive. The lawyer is on it, DeSimone will do the best that can be done. All this is out of our hands, so ain't no need in crying over spilled milk."

As Uncle Ray Ray was speaking on behalf of Nard, he heard someone at the door. It was Crystal, and to say the least, time had changed her, so much so that Beverly didn't know if she was coming or going. The only thing that was still stable was Tyrone. For the first time, in all the years they had been together, she could honestly say that their relationship was solid, like a rock. Tyrone was still right there, right by her side. He had moved in, fully committed to her and their relationship. He got a job down at a steel factory in South Philly and was a hard-working man, doing the right thing by her.

Her cousin Chris, oh, jeez, this fool was caught trying to break into their house. And he had been snatching old ladies' purses, taking their ATM cards and trying to figure out their bank card codes to withdraw their money from the ATM. You would think he would have known he was on camera standing at the ATM machine, but he didn't. So he had many charges of theft and burglary, and Uncle Ray Ray kept bailing him out of prison. He was so thin and frail, he just looked bad. Beverly felt sorry for Uncle Ray Ray. He had tears in his eyes every time he saw his son.

"What in the world is wrong with this boy? I've done the best I can. There is nothing I can do with him," explained Uncle Ray Ray to Sergeant Wright as they watched the police manhandle a fighting, yelling, kicking, and screaming Chris into the back of a police car after Mr. Clarence spotted a man in the alleyway in the back of their house. Not knowing it was Chris, Mr. Clarence had called the police, looking out for Ray and Beverly. When the police arrived they caught Chris climbing through a window that he had broken in the back of the house that led into the basement. It was really sad, but worse than Chris was Crystal. She had turned out to be the neighborhood crack whore and Uncle Ray Ray, Beverly, Donna, Maeleen, and Rev all had to witness her life crumble in front of them. Crystal really let herself go and Beverly couldn't help her.

"Here she go, right here, I told you she'd show up..."

"Crystal?" Beverly asked, cutting her uncle right off.

"Mmm-hmm, the one and only," he answered peering out at her, not sure if he should open the door.

"Where's them papers I need her to sign?" asked Beverly, tired of Crystal and her games. She had gotten strung out on crack cocaine real bad. All she did was get high. They said she sold her body out at Cobbs Creek Park in Southwest Philly where she had moved with her momma. She was thin and raggedy-looking, her hair was never done, just pulled back, and her teeth were turning a dark yellow-gray color. Her clothes stayed dirty, and whenever she wanted something she showed up at Beverly's door, where she had abandoned Dayanna shortly after she started getting high with her momma and her momma's boyfriend. Beverly heard through the grapevine that it was the mother's boyfriend who got the mother turned out first, and then the mother turned a blind eye when the boyfriend went after Crystal and started getting her high so he could have sex with her. All the mother cared about was getting her daily doses of crack cocaine. As long as she was straight, she didn't care what happened to Crystal, and that's how it was. Crystal was staying inside a crack house off of Fifty-seventh and Webster Street. Beverly knew that if Nard could see her now, he wouldn't believe she was his baby's mother. Crystal used her pretty looks to get her high, but her looks didn't last long chasing after Mr. Gusto, and once the streets got hold of her, she was done. Beverly's only concern was for her grandbaby, Dayanna, whom she and Uncle Ray Ray had taken in and cared for now for over a year and a half. You couldn't tell Beverly that wasn't her baby. You couldn't tell Uncle Ray Ray the baby wasn't his either. Both felt the same, and Crystal better not even think she would be taking that baby out of that house and away from them, especially the way she looked and was carrying on in the streets. She could stop by and see the baby but Dayanna wasn't going anywhere.

Uncle Ray Ray opened the door, letting her in. She looked angry and jittery, and smelled like burned sulfur. The scent lingered in the air, radiating off her body.

"Where's my baby?" she asked with an air of entitlement.

"Donna got her. She took her and Mia to the park."

Beverly took the papers her uncle handed her that she needed Crystal to sign. Crystal wasn't a mother, she was too young and too selfish to be a mother, and now with her drug addiction she couldn't really care less, and did nothing for Dayanna. It was sad to see women willing to sell everything, including their bodies and their young, but Beverly knew in her heart that Crystal would sell her soul just to get high off crack. She saw it firsthand living in North Philadelphia. The neighborhood had turned into a war zone, between the drug dealers fighting over the various blocks and the crackheads running around robbing everybody, nobody and nothing was safe. The block was changing because the people were changing. It was the spring of 1988 and the city was on fire, exploding with a flood of drugs and guns on the streets.

"Crystal, I need you to sign these papers, 'cause I don't think you understand, but I ain't called nobody on you leaving this child, 'cause I don't want to see them lock your ass up, but I got things to do. You not gonna take care of that baby. Somebody has to feed her, clothe her, and provide for her, but I need some assistance and you ain't doing nothing."

"And neither is Nard, he ain't never did nothing to help me."

She was a real crackhead, and talking to her was a complete waste of Beverly's time.

"Look, the baby is under this roof, and I need legal guardianship, do you understand? The lady down at the state office building said for you to sign her over and they would be able to give me assistance."

"Well, what you giving me?" a skinny, nasty mouthed Crystal spat back at Beverly.

"Girl, ain't nothing to give you, I'm taking care of your baby. You should be giving me something."

"Well, I need some money and I'll sign your papers."

"How much money?" Beverly asked, looking at her.

"Umm, a hundred dollars," said Crystal, dreaming of how high she could get with that.

"I don't have no hundred dollars, is you crazy?" Beverly pulled out the money she had in her back pocket, fifty-three dollars.

"Here, it's yours, fifty-three dollars, you can have it."

Beverly watched as Crystal took the papers out of her hand and signed over legal guardianship to Beverly just as Donna opened the door, busting through with Dayanna, who was almost three and was walking and talking like she knew exactly what was going on. Holding the door, Donna let Mia and Dayanna through the doorway before she followed them close behind.

Crystal passed the papers back to Beverly and Beverly handed her the fifty-three dollars. Donna watched as Crystal counted the money and stuffed it in her back pocket. Crystal turned, picking up her daughter.

"Hey, munchkin, you know I miss you, right, I do, I do," she cooed to the toddler before putting her down and leaving so quickly she didn't even say good-bye.

"That girl is on drugs," said Donna, looking at Crystal as she walked by her and out the door, fifty-three dollars richer.

Beverly and Donna followed Crystal outside and watched her walk down the street. It would be the last time they would ever see Crystal. She would never return.

"She is a hot mess. It's so sad that girl messed her life up like that. She really don't make no sense," said Beverly, shaking her head. "At least I finally got my papers signed and I can go ahead and get the legal guardianship squared away with the courts and get my welfare assistance and medical."

"Yeah, get on that right away." Donna nodded as she spotted her brother Rev across the street.

"You know Maeleen's pregnant, right? She done came outside from a long cold winter with her belly sticking out."

"No, you lying," said Donna, knowing now that her brother

Rev would end up with Maeleen for the rest of his life.

"I seen her yesterday. I meant to call and tell you. Her and Rev is having a baby."

Donna called her brother from across the street. Rev came over all smiles, just as happy as he could be.

"How y'all feeling on this beautiful spring day?" asked Rev, hugging and kissing them both.

Donna jumped right on her brother for not letting her know that Maeleen was pregnant.

"Yeah, it's like another miracle 'cause Maeleen's tubes were supposed to be tied."

Donna and Beverly looked at each other, knowing that the unimaginable was imaginable with Maeleen.

"Her tubes are tied and she's pregnant?" questioned Donna as Maeleen walked up on the conversation.

"Rev, you gonna fix the doorknob or just let it fall off?" Maeleen asked, bossing him back to work as usual.

"Yeah, woman, I got that. I've got work to do, y'all," he said, taking Maeleen by the arm and kissing her cheek. "Girl, your skin is so soft it's like rubbing on a rabbit," said Rev, rubbing Maeleen's arm, smiling as if he were the luckiest man in the world.

He ran off and Maeleen, Donna, and Beverly watched him go back across the street.

"Your skin is beautiful, Maeleen. What kind of lotion you be using?" asked Beverly, ready to go out and buy some.

"Ain't no lotion, I pee in the bath water just like my grandmomma told me to."

"Aww, Maeleen, tell me you not over there doing that nasty shit," said Donna, not feeling like hearing this crazy bitch and her bullshit today.

"I'm trying to tell you, all you got to do is pee in your bath water and your skin will be so soft, just like a newborn baby," she said, smiling and rubbing herself.

"Maeleen, don't start. Ain't nobody peein' in no bath water and sittin' in it," said Beverly.

"Well, I do, and that's why that nigga's over there right now, waiting to rub on my soft ass, okay? Shit, I don't know why I waste my time even comin' over here on this side of the damn street anyway. And I'm trying to help you the fuck out," she said in her usual manner, cussing them out for the block to hear as she walked down the porch steps. "Oh, but you awake, right?" she asked, turning around and facing Beverly, eye to eye. "How many fingers am I holding up, Beverly?"

"Three," Beverly responded.

"That's what I thought," Maeleen yelled, holding up her entire hand like Ike Turner as she flagged them both, deciding that she didn't want to be bothered with the two of them.

"Hey, Maeleen, how you feeling today?" asked Uncle Ray Ray, opening the screen door holding a pitcher of half and half.

"I'm all right, how you?" she asked him right back, standing in the middle of the street. She had had a soft spot for Ray every since Beverly was shot and was in the hospital.

"I'm good, I got some ribs in the oven if you want some," he said, willing to feed her any day of the week. In his heart, he believed that if not for her, Beverly wouldn't be here today. Beverly thought he was just as crazy as Maeleen and sat there frowning along with Donna as they looked at Ray, Maeleen, and then each other, shaking their heads.

"All right I'm gonna cut me up a chicken and I'll get some ribs later, Ray."

Everyone watched Maeleen cross the street and walk back up her own stoop.

"You know she talking about cutting up one of those chickens she got in her backyard, right?" asked Beverly in all seriousness as they watched Maeleen walking down the sidewalk.

"If that crazy bitch don't go get some Perdue and stop playing with me," joked Donna, already knowing about Maeleen and all the chickens she kept in the back of her house, in a tiny box space next to the alleyway.

"Mmm-hmm, you sure are friendly with Maeleen, Ray Ray," joked Donna.

"Don't worry about who I'm friendly with. I'm just fine. Hey, y'all, let's play some spades," smiled Ray, ready to get a game going.

"Come on, you can't beat me, Ray," said Donna.

"Shut up, both y'all. You know you lose your dirty drawers coming up against me," joked Ray as he grabbed a deck of cards off a side table on the porch. "Come on, let me show you who the man is around here. Hit me!"

2006

EYES FREE

It was February of 2006 and Nard was up for another parole hearing. *Motherfuckers ain't gots to let me go no god damn where. I'm fine right here, you fucking bloodsuckers.* He spat into the toilet before zipping up his pants, then flushing. Nard stood in his cell talking to himself and thinking about the young man he once was when he came through the doors of Green, seemingly to never be released. He thought back to that dreary, cold, rainy day when he stood before the prison system's hearing officer, who acted as a judge, and was resentenced all over again. His new sentence was fifteen to twenty-five, just as DeSimone predicted. He would never forget faggot-ass Smitty as long as he lived, Hawk, or Otis, and while he had gotten his revenge on each and every last one of them, revenge had a price. It cost him time. A lot of time, just like that bitch-ass Daisy Mae Fothergill. He wished he could get his hands on her. He dreamed of her every night and thought about her every day. He remembered her on the stand like it was yesterday. He would never forget that day as long as he lived. *That bitch…she fucked everything up. If I could get my hands on that bitch right now, damn!* He couldn't help but think what he'd do.

Flashes of strangling her, fucking her, then strangling her to death over and over and over never went away, and the feeling still hadn't faded. *At least I got Otis's fat ass and his faggot-ass crew.* He smiled at his thoughts, remembering the day he whooped Smitty's ass to death. *Mmm-hmm, motherfucker, that's what the fuck you get. Payback, bitch.*

Smitty had had his back to him as Nard walked into his cell. He had watched Smitty's cellmate roll out, making his way out to the yard. With his back turned, Smitty never saw Nard coming or his death that was right around the corner. He had just finished using the toilet in his cell, zipped up his institutional khakis, and flushed the toilet when he felt someone in his space.

He turned around quickly, blocking the wooden blade Nard was wielding. With the smoothness of an experienced street fighter, Smitty grabbed Nard's free hand as he blocked the knife with his other hand. Smitty knocked the wooden shank out of Nard's hand. He drove his fist into Nard's small, young frame with an uppercut, to his midsection, but just when he thought he had Nard where he wanted him, cradled on the floor, Nard fooled him and was up again, wooden shank in hand, as he pummeled Smitty and stabbed him repeatedly until he fell to the floor.

Smitty, unable to breathe as blood began to gurgle out of his mouth, lay on his cell floor in excruciating pain, with Nard on top of him like a wild jungle cat, just as his crew walked down the block and saw Nard going in.

"Yo, man, what the fuck you doing?" asked Otis, as he took his fist and knocked Nard in the side of his head. Nard fell on the floor as Otis fell on top of him, landing punch after punch on Nard's upper body. But Nard had the wooden shank, and he took on Otis and another guy who seemingly came from behind

Nard and joined in the fight. By the time Nard was done, Smitty was dead, and he was holding some guy's eyeball in his hand as two COs were standing in the middle of the block facing the cell, with their guns aimed and ready to fire.

"Drop your weapon and move slowly out of the cell with your hands behind your back," said one of the COs.

The fighting stopped, and Nard realized that he was covered in blood, whose he didn't know, but it wasn't his. He looked down at the men sprawled across the cell. He dropped the wooden shank in his right hand and Otis's squished eyeball from his left hand, put his hands behind his head, and began to walk slowly out of the cell as he had been instructed. Several correctional officers tackled him. After he was handcuffed behind his back, they dragged him from the floor, with Otis screaming in pain at the realization that his eyeball was gone.

"See if you see that, motherfucker! Huh, I bet you wish you never fucked with me! You lucky I don't kill you," Nard screamed, kicking his legs as he was dragged away by the two COs while other officers were assisting the injured inside the cell.

Little did Nard know, but he would be charged with murder and attempted murder and then placed in the hole so long he wouldn't remember daylight, and for the past twenty years, he hadn't.

The three men behind the desk in front of him looked at one another as they sat there evaluating Bernard Guess for possible parole. All they were doing was the same thing they had done the last six times he was up for parole, asking Nard the same ol' stupid-ass questions with a red rubber denied stamp in their hands.

"Are you sorry for what you did?"

No, no the fuck I'm not.

"Why did you kill those two men on Somerset Street?"

Because it was the right thing to do?

"Why did you squeeze your victim's eyeball?"

So that motherfucker would never see me coming.

That seemed to be why he was continually denied, Otis's god damn eyeball. Forget the fact that he had killed a man, the parole board just couldn't get past him squeezing Otis's eyeball. It ruined his parole chances every time.

Ain't this some shit? They still harpin' on that. This nigga's eyeball could have me in here for fucking ever.

"Are you sorry for what you did?"

No, bitch, no the fuck I'm not. I'm glad I killed Smitty before he killed me and I'm glad I whooped Otis's ass, stabbed up the other two and squished the man's eyeball. And if you let me out this motherfucker and I see any of them niggas in the street, I'm gonna try to knock all their eyeballs out their head and squish them again as best I can, he thought before he responded.

"Yes, ma'am, of course I'm sorry, who wouldn't be, it's cost me my life, ma'am. *These white folks is killing me with all these questions. They can just let me go on about my day. I got shit to do in this motherfucker.* And he did, Nard worked in the kitchen, so he always had the extra food for favors. Not to mention a championship chess tournament, and of course, the chess king himself was playing. He looked at the clock on the wall and then back to the hearing officers. They just wouldn't stop. *Please, white people, please, my chess game is about to start.*

All those questions, just wasting time as Nard's mind wandered back to his block. He looked at the clock on the wall again, feeling so impatient he was ready to burst out of the door and haul his ass back to his cell. *I have got to go. I got a game, man.*

He sat with his hands folded in front of him in his lap wearing his state-issued blues as he jittered his leg, tapping his foot on the floor. He had on a pair of dark navy blue pants and a light blue button-down shirt.

"Do you think if you are let back into society you will commit another act of violence?"

Yes, ma'am, yes I will. And that's my final answer! He laughed to himself, thinking of his new favorite game show. *Bitch, let me out this motherfucker so we can see.*

Every night and every day Nard would search in his mind how he ended up in prison for so long. *That bitch Daisy and her fucking testimony.* Truth was he wasn't a fool, he could count time. He should have been home back in 1988 instead of being found guilty of murder for Smitty's fat ass and attempted murder for the rest of those guys, especially after what they did to him. At least he got respect for sitting in that hole for three years and coming out head still strong. The hole can break you mentally, but it didn't break Nard. Every day he got himself through, every night he dreamed himself freedom. And more than often, he dreamed of the day he'd get his revenge on that Daisy bitch who sold him down the river like a broken-down slave. Had she just given the testimony she was supposed to, he'd never have gone to jail in the first place. At least that's how he saw it. After being denied parole six times, he never imagined seven would be his lucky number. Two weeks later, his counselor broke the news.

"I already spoke with Ms. Gotling from the halfway house. She said she'll have a bed ready for you next week. Isn't that great, looks like you're outta here on the seventh of February, just in time for Valentine's."

His counselor smiled, happy and excited about his release. What could be better than going home? For some reason, Nard couldn't answer that question. For him, it didn't feel better. Nard faced his counselor as he stamped some papers, passed Nard a copy, initialed others, and kept moving paper. Nard wanted to join in the celebration, but for some strange reason, he wasn't elated. He was somber, as if the news was someone else's and not his own.

"What's the matter? Why aren't you happy?" asked his counselor, noticing Nard looked as if he had just lost his best friend.

"I don't know what to say. I'm a little shocked, I guess." Nard responded politely. The truth was he was scared to death. He didn't know what he was going to do. Where he was going to go or how he would take care of himself. Of course he was happy to be going home, to have freedom and to be with his family, but after that, he knew the cold reality of what lay ahead. He had spent the last half of his life in jail, and at forty-two years old, he had no idea what lay ahead for him, and the thought of what life had in store was bleak. He heard guys talking all the time about when they would be released, only to find themselves right back in prison, usually in less than a year. Most of them couldn't make it out of the halfway house, let alone function in society, and in most cases they ended up right back on the block. Most of the guys said the same thing. No one would give them a job, no one would give them a chance, all because of their criminal record. Especially the violent offenders; they could forget it. No one wanted a violent person in the workplace. Life was already stressful enough, can you imagine having someone who was capable of doing harm, on the job? Absolutely not! And if they were to find work, they would have to lie about their criminal history to get the job. But once the employer did a background search, FIRED! So, there you had it. No job meant no money, no money meant no livelihood, no livelihood meant no reason to care. He went back to his cell, which he shared with a guy named Merlin Watkins. Merlin and Nard had become thick as thieves. Nard was okay with Merlin, even if he did talk in his sleep a lot. That Merlin knew his entire life story. He shared his good fortune at making parole with literally everyone he came in contact with, vowing never to see them again.

The seventh wasn't far away, just around the corner. Actually the time passed so quickly, Nard wasn't prepared to leave. He quickly finished packing his box as Merlin helped him. Two correctional officers came to the cell, looked in, and asked him if he was ready. Nard had promised to keep in touch with Merlin, but Merlin knew he'd probably never hear from him again. Nard followed them quietly, taking his last walk down the hall. *I won't miss it, not one bit. Good riddance!* The correctional officers led Nard downstairs to the discharge unit. He was given his personal belongings and was allowed to change into the suit he had been wearing when he was sent to prison. They cashed a state-issued check for forty-three dollars, which was what they gave every inmate upon his release. And that was it, they were kicking him out.

The time seemed like it had flown by, a long, hard bid, but he couldn't believe that he had spent the last twenty years locked away. *It's all that bitch's fault.* And while the long, hard road of incarceration was now behind him, in his mind, he was still trapped in a cell.

Transferred to the halfway house down in North Philly on Twelfth and Lehigh Avenue, he was led inside by his sheriff escorts.

"Here you go, Ms. Gotling. I got another one for you," said one of the sheriffs as he signed off on some paperwork, passed it to the woman standing before him, watched as she signed it, then turned and walked away.

"Have a good one," he said, closing the door behind him.

A ruckus could be heard out in the hallway as Luis, one of the guys who worked at the halfway house, was arguing with a parolee.

"It's not my fault, man, what do you want me to do?"

"You taking my stuff, that's my stuff."

"Hey, Hector, calm down, he's just doing his job. You know the rules. You got caught and you're going back to jail," said Ms. Gotling, tough as nails.

Ms. Gotling was having Hector Gonzales arrested for violating his parole. Hector had been caught with a cell phone. This fool was talking to his girlfriend at one o'clock in the morning. His love for Maria Consquela would now cost him his freedom. Yup, back to jail for our buddy Hector, all because he couldn't sleep and wanted to hear her voice.

"Please, Ms. Gotling, please, please, I swear to God, please, just one more chance."

"No, you know the rules. Get him out of here," she ordered the two sheriffs dressed in green uniforms who were there to escort Hector's pleading ass right on back to jail.

"Next!" she hollered, like a general leading in combat.

"My name is Bernard Guess, I've been transferred fr—"

Nard couldn't get another word out before Ms. Gotling cut him off. "I know who you are; sit back down," she commanded as she walked back into the intake office. Nard didn't know who this woman thought she was talking to but he wasn't going back to jail, so he sat down as he was told. Ms. Gotling ran him through the procedures at the halfway house and made it perfectly clear if he didn't have a job in two weeks, he'd be going back to jail.

"Do you understand, Mr. Guess?"

"Yes, ma'am," said Nard, being as polite as any gentleman could be.

"That's what they all say, and yet I have the sheriff's number on speed dial waiting to escort all of you back upstate. I don't understand it. You guys taste freedom and forget you're still state property. I suggest you follow the house rules or you'll be just like him, going back to where you came from. You catch my drift, Mr. Guess?"

"Yeah, I catch it," answered Nard, looking at Ms. Gotling and wondering why no one had found her naked body mangled, tied up, and locked away in a closet somewhere. *Speed dial if you want to, bitch, see how this shit goes down.*

She called out for Luis, who was nursing a scratch on his arm from Hector Gonzales.

"Would you take Mr. Guess here and show him his bed. He's 3B." She watched as Nard got up and walked out the door, following closely behind Luis.

I'll give him two months tops, she thought, betting with herself as she did with most inmates who came through the door.

Nard would be sharing room B with three other guys. He was bed three. He sat down, testing out the mattress. It felt better than the hard metal bunk he was used to sleeping on. Actually, it was quite soft. He didn't have much to unpack, but there was a tiny floor dresser with two drawers at the foot of the bed. Luis showed him the house. They ate and did their laundry in the basement. They were free to go from 7:00 a.m. to 7:00 p.m. unless they had night work; then they would be given different schedules.

"Make sure you're back every night at seven o'clock or she'll send you back to jail, my friend. Trust me, I see it every day," said Luis, giving Nard the best advice he could think of.

In the social room there was plenty of seating, televisions, tables, and chairs, and it was where everyone gathered. Off to the side there was a telephone and a pen and pad.

"Always a line for the phone, I can't never make a call when I need to. Shit, I might as well sign my name, too," said a guy standing behind Nard who was waiting to sign the phone sign-in sheet. "How you feeling, brother, my name is Quinny, but everybody calls me Quinny Day. You just get here, brother?"

"Yeah, today," Nard said, shaking the guy's hand and welcoming the introduction.

"Well, I can tell you now, Ms. Gotling, that bitch, is on some straight bullshit. All she do is lock niggas back up every day for nothing. I think she must get some kind of extra bonus in her paycheck or something 'cause don't nobody make it out this motherfucker. I got two more months left, and trust me, you got to stay one step ahead of Ms. Gotling or she'll get ya."

"Two months?"

"Yeah, state can't hold you in this motherfucker but for six. I done did four and I'm telling you that bitch right there be trying to set me up every chance she can get. But she can't get me," he whispered as Ms. Gotling walked around the corner. "You looking mighty lovely today, Ms. Gotling, is that a new hairdo?"

"Don't worry about how I look, you just worry about yourself," Ms. Gotling snapped as she walked past them and down the long hallway.

"Bitch," he whispered as he watched her. "Who's fucking her? Who is fucking this bitch? That's all I want to know? 'Cause that's one evil white woman and whoever he is, he need his ass kicked, for real," said Quinny Day, smiling as he passed the pen back to Nard. Nard looked down the sheet. There were at least fifteen names before his.

"Don't worry, people be signing but they don't stick around. It won't take that long, old head," joked Quinny Day.

Old head, who's he calling old head? Nard wondered if he really was looking that old.

It was no wonder Hector was going back to jail. If this is what you had to go through to make a call, Nard understood why the guy got caught with a cell phone.

"Why don't they get more than one phone?"

"Then niggas wouldn't need to sneak on cell phones. Shit is a trap to lock you back up, that's all," said Quinny Day, giving Nard the science and the math to the bullshit they were up against.

The two sat in the "social room," as Ms. Gotling called it, waiting for the phone. Nard wanted to call home and let his mother know where he had been transferred to. Now that he was back in the city, it was nothing but a train and a bus ride to get back home. He'd be over tomorrow after he followed through on his job search. Ms. Gotling already had three job interviews lined up for him. So he was hopeful, really hopeful.

"You stick with me, old head, I'll tell you what to do to get out this halfway house. You'll be home in no time."

"She said if I don't get a job, I'd be back in jail in two weeks," Nard said, wondering what he was going to do.

"Yeah, and how you gonna get a job? You think they just gonna give you one? You better get down with ShopRite. At least that bitch can't send you back to jail," said Quinny, shaking his head as if he knew he was right.

"Packaging groceries?"

"Yeah, you can go in there tomorrow and be working the same day."

"Bagging groceries?"

"Yeah, why not?"

"'Cause, I ain't doing that bullshit. You must be crazy."

"Okay, well, I take it with your Harvard degree and long history of work experience, you'll be working for a Fortune 500 company in no time, huh?" asked Quinny in all seriousness. "Old head, you better stop playing with these white folks out here and go get you a job at ShopRite. It's right down the street, you can walk to work. It's either that or street sweeping. And shit, it's cold outside, what you gonna do?"

Nard couldn't believe those were his only two choices, packing up groceries for tips or sweeping the streets with one of those street-sweeping machines.

"There has to be better jobs out there than that," he said, looking at Quinny Day like he was crazy.

"There is, but ain't nobody giving them to you, old head. You must've done bumped your head. You're a felon, you ain't never getting no good job. So, to get out this halfway house, you gonna have to pay six months of dues, but trust me, it'll be worth it. These motherfuckers out here ain't got shit for you, but ShopRite," said Quinny Day, as if he knew exactly what he was talking about. "Let me know, I can get you an application from my boss and bring it home to you. I been there for the past four months, old head, bagging my groceries, minding my business, and I come sit in here every night and watch the news, *Law & Order Special Victims Unit*, and Ms. Gotling locking somebody back up, every night, but it ain't me. I'm just telling you, six months, you can do it, man."

The next day, Nard took the list of places Ms. Gotling told him that he was to go. Nothing was how he remembered it. He realized how the movement of the streets echoed on, far past his reach. Jail had somehow warped him from the movement of time and even though the streets were still there, Broad Street, Germantown Avenue, Lehigh Avenue, Susquehanna, Dauphin, they didn't look the way he remembered them. Faces of strangers even looked odd to him at first, everybody was Muslim now, no more dope games. It was a different game, a different pace, and Nard felt just a little out of place. Identifying himself was harder when he looked in the mirror real good for the first time. Bright light showed the speckling of gray strands here and there on his face. While he at least could say he had kept himself in shape, his shell had truly aged. Prison had wearied and worried him, and he could see it now, really see it when he looked in the mirror at the reflection of his face. It was even worse for him when he looked outside at all that was around him. Everything had changed from what he remembered from twenty years ago. Even watching the people walk down the street was different. The way they dressed was different. Nobody had Jheri curls anymore; he saw not a one. But best believe the women were now wearing weaves, and the ones that weren't wearing weaves were garbed and covered. The ghetto looked harder, with rows of dilapidated buildings. His halfway house was a few blocks from Broad on Lehigh, but closer to Germantown, and it was torn down. There were a lot of abandoned buildings and a lot of people strung out on drugs, like crack, heroin, and pills. Syrup was still a big seller in the city, as was "wet." Nard saw the way the hustle was going down and how the young kids were deep in the gangs, but not the gangs he knew of. These were the new-school Bloods and new-school Crips. Nard was back on his Streets 101 classes every time he stepped out of the door.

He thought of the look on his mother's face when she opened the door and saw him, a free man for the first time in twenty years. Her smile spread wide and the same open arms she always had for him found themselves finally holding her son.

"He's here, my baby's home," she yelled, as everyone jumped from around the corners into the foyer and yelled, "Welcome home," in unison, as if they had been practicing all day.

It was the nicest homecoming anyone could have asked for. Everybody was there, Beverly, Tyrone, Donna, her new man, Carl, and her three foster kids. Of course Uncle Ray Ray was there, his son Chris, and even Maeleen and Rev were there.

"Mia, this is my dad," said Dayanna, hugging Nard as her girlfriend extended her hand. "Hi, Mr. Guess," she said, as Beverly watched the girls. They were both attractive, both bright, and both boy crazy. Beverly remembered her obscure teenage days and raging hormones. Now, nothing was obscure, wearing jeans and UGG boots and tight thermal long-sleeved shirts, the girls sat down in the corner and began their usual "club house" gossip. It was here at home that Nard began to feel comfortable with familiarity. It was also here that Nard found out about Crystal, that she had gone on to have three more crack babies, and how bad she was still strung out on drugs. After all these years, Nard couldn't believe she was still getting high. He still yearned to see her, though, crackhead or not. After dinner, Nard had to get going, he had a seven o'clock curfew and he couldn't be late. He knew the rules.

Beverly and Tyrone stood at the door, as people filed out behind one another. "It's cold out here," said Beverly, closing the door behind Rev and Maeleen.

"Close the door!" snapped Uncle Ray.

"I am, Uncle Ray Ray, just settle down," said Beverly to her sixty-six-year-old uncle, who was driving her more and more crazy the older he got.

"You want a blanket, Uncle Ray?" asked Tyrone, holding a crocheted baby blue blanket that Beverly had picked up at a yard sale out in Lancaster County for three dollars.

"I might as well, she's trying to freeze me in here. She knows

I'm old," said Uncle Ray, glad Tyrone was around. Tyrone placed the blanket on Uncle Ray and covered his feet, tucking the blanket under them just like his mother used to do for him as a child.

"There you go, Uncle Ray, you should warm up now."

Beverly walked into the family room where her uncle was watching television and sat down on the sofa.

"I'm going to take a shower and lie down, I got work in the morning," said Tyrone, leaving the two of them alone together as Beverly waved him on.

"Nard seems different, don't he, Uncle Ray?"

Uncle Ray Ray had aged over the years. He had his ups and downs with his gout and had to watch his diet. He needed glasses now, and Beverly kept telling him that he had to get a hearing aid, but other than moving a little slower, he was still good to go.

"What you expect, twenty years, anybody would be different. That boy did hard time, shit, they kept him in the damn hole half the time he was locked up. He knocked one guy's eye out his head and damn near ate some other guy's ear." Uncle Ray stopped for a moment and looked at his niece in all seriousness. "He's changed, I just ain't figured out what it is he's changed into."

MONEY, MONEY, MONEY

Every single person from human resources with whom he interviewed said the same thing.

"I'm sorry, you just don't have enough experience."

They had a hundred and one reasons not to hire him. If they didn't say he didn't have enough experience, they said that the position was filled already or the position was already taken, and of course they all finished with the same last line, "But, we'll keep your application on file and call you if something opens up."

He had heard only rejection at his ill-fated attempts to find gainful employment. He was running out of options, and before he lost his freedom again, he decided it would be best to mosey down to ShopRite and fill out an application.

Sitting at the table, he watched the store's manager scribbling notes as he glanced at Nard, then his application.

"You can start immediately?" the manager, Mr. Henley, asked.

"Yeah, right now if you want me to," said Nard, not having much to do.

"No, come in tomorrow. You have to be here at eleven o'clock every night. Can you do that, eleven to seven?"

"Yes, sir," answered Nard, as if pulling an all-nighter was a walk in the park.

"Um, excuse me, sir. How much does the job pay?" Nard asked wondering what kind of money he'd be making.

"Six dollars and fifty cents per hour," said Mr. Henley, as if a man could survive on that.

Nard quietly counted in his head. And if that wasn't enough, he heard Mr. Henley in the distance speaking to the assistant manager as he was leaving.

"I hired a new stockboy. He starts tomorrow."

It was a fact, Nard was ShopRite's newest stockboy. Fortunately for him, he had to work the night shift, which was even better. He could work all night and be in an empty halfway house sleeping all day and talking on the phone. The lines in the phone room weren't as long during the day as they were in the evening when everyone was around. *A ShopRite stockboy, I can't believe these white folks got me doing this bullshit.* And he really couldn't. It was unfathomable, to say the least. But, what choice did he have? None! So stocking shelves at ShopRite became his livelihood. He was able to build a tight little ShopRite stash with most of the money he made. If not for Dayanna, who claimed she needed child support, he would have been all right. She had a hundred and one excuses for why she really needed the money, too, from her hair to her nails. She requested money to go to the movies, or the mall, and was seemingly needy regarding everything she yapped about out of her twenty-year-old mouth. He worked faithfully every night, five nights a week, in that wretched grocery store. He at times seemed tormented by his past. And while he had now been home for over three months, he hadn't found anyone to spend his time with. And it wasn't that he wasn't trying, either. Every Friday when he got paid, he'd hit the local bar in the neighborhood, sometimes he'd venture down South Street for a few hours before curfew. He was always polite to the ladies, always offered to buy them a drink, tried basic conversation, but not being the most attractive man on the planet, and with a night job at ShopRite, no car, no dough, and residing in a halfway house after spending half of his life in prison wasn't exactly getting him any closer to a one-night stand or a relationship. Actually, no one seemed interested in him past casual conversation, and only two women had given him real numbers, but every time he called them, they were busy.

Tired of being rejected in bars and clubs and wasting his hard-earned weekly money and getting nothing but blue balls, he retreated downtown to an XXX shop that sold videos and sexual devices and offered peep shows. It had become a weekly tradition of sorts. He'd leave the halfway house a little early before he had to go to work and hop the train to center city, making sure to be at ShopRite by eleven.

Four months later the day was slowly approaching that he'd be able to leave the halfway house and move home to his mother's. He couldn't wait. No more bitch-ass Ms. Gotling and no more worrying about being sent back to prison. She was hell on earth, the gatekeeper for Satan himself. He saw exactly how viciously the game of freedom was being played. It was just three weeks before Quinny Day was supposed to be released from the halfway house when his mother collapsed, suffering a fatal heart attack. Quinny stayed by her side, rushing her to the emergency room with the EMT workers. With his mother barely alive, he left her side to return to the halfway house, unable to reach Ms. Gotling. Taking a hack instead of the train, he got jammed on the Roosevelt and was thirty-seven minutes late. Ms. Gotling was waiting and so were the sheriffs.

"Yo, be easy, man, my mother had a heart attack and I been at the hospital with her. Look, I even got a note and a copy of her intake sheet for you. I even tried to call you, but you didn't pick up," said Quinny, shrugging his shoulders at her as if there was nothing he could do. Literally, what could he do—his mother had had a heart attack.

"You know the rules," she said sternly.

"Oh, no, tell me you not, I got three weeks, three fucking weeks and I get to go home," he said, his tone now changing.

"Sheriffs!" she called out, and from out of the side room they immediately appeared, ready to whisk him away as if his life and his mother's life meant nothing.

"Yo, bitch, hold the fuck up, what the fuck is wrong with you, my moms had a heart attack, look at the paper, look at the paper. I been at the hospital."

She turned her head quickly and faced him, "I don't care where you've been. You broke curfew, you know the rules."

For one split second Nard's eyes met Quinny's. The words broken, destroyed, and devastated would not adequately define or describe the look on that man's face.

Nard thought Quinny was going to pounce on Ms. Gotling like a cougar attacking his prey and rip her heart out, if she had one. Nard couldn't believe it, and that wasn't the only time. She sent a black man back to prison every other week for some bullshit. One guy got sent back to prison 'cause he couldn't find a job.

"Too bad, you know the deal. I told you to find a job," she'd snap without blinking.

It was sad, and the bad part was, Quinny was a good guy. He simply had one thing that hindered him. He stuttered. It wasn't his fault, it just wasn't working out for him on those job interviews, especially sounding out his words when he was nervous. Nard watched as Quinny started crying and pleading with the gatekeeper, Ms. Gotling. It was no use; she had the sheriffs there ready and waiting. Nard looked on as the sheriffs escorted Quinny away and back to jail, like it was nothing, all because his momma had a heart attack and he had taken her to the hospital.

"Yo, homie, I got you. I'll tell your sister what happened," said Nard as the sheriffs grabbed Quinny's arms and walked him down the hall. Nard already knew that it would be days before Quinny could get to a phone. His family would be sick with worry because, of course, among all the things that Ms. Gotling had to do to lock a nigga up for nothing, she didn't have to notify next of kin, family, or friends. Poor Quinny, he'd do nine months before getting in front of the parole board to explain what happened to his momma and how she died five days later. Of course, they would decide that under the circumstances it would be appropriate to void the incident from his record and allow him to be released again. But because of the overcrowding caused by the number of inmates being released into halfway houses and the lack of facilities, there weren't enough beds. Unfortunately, Quinny would sit in prison another six months waiting for a bed even though the parole board had found in his favor. Nard would never forget prison or the halfway house as long as he lived. He would never believe the operation they had set in place and how he had been used for free labor. He would never forget what happened to him. He had nightmares and dreams to remind him every night.

Officially, he was still on parole, but he had made the six months work for him. And now that he was home all he had to do was report to his parole officer within ten days of leaving the halfway house. He had no more curfew, no more anything. All he had to do was stay clean and check in at his parole office on his assigned days.

Beverly was happy to have her son back home with her. It was the middle of August and they decided to have a barbecue to celebrate in the backyard. Family and friends gathered, celebrating and toasting Nard's homecoming.

"You home now, son. Glad to have you back." Uncle Ray Ray gave Nard a welcome-home hug, let him go, and patted him on the back. "To new beginnings," he said as he held up a glass and toasted his nephew's homecoming.

Now free from the halfway house, and able to venture out without a curfew, Nard had a few places and a few people he needed to track down. The first on his list was Sticks. And even though he had been as good as dead for over twenty years now, Nard still needed to go back to where he had left off. He wanted to go to where his friend Sticks used to live. He remembered the block like the back of his hand. He had grown up there, playing basketball every day in the park around the corner, running to Sticks's house for ice pops or needing fifty cents for the ice cream truck.

"Who is it?" asked Kay Ross.

"It's me, Ms. Ross, Nard, Sticks's old friend," said Nard, wondering if the family even still lived there. A few seconds later, he heard the chain pop and the locks turn, and the door opened. A tiny, elderly, frail woman opened the door.

"Nard, is that you? Boy, you done turned into an old man," she said, smiling from ear to ear and letting him inside.

"Yes, ma'am, I sure have," he said, happy to see the closest thing to his best friend.

"It's been many, many years," said Ms. Ross as she sat Nard down in a chair by the television. "You want some tea? Or some coffee?" she asked.

"Um, no, ma'am, I'm okay. You know, I always think about Sticks. He was my best friend."

"Mine, too, not a day goes by I don't think of him either." She smiled.

The two shared stories going back some thirty years, and for that short while, Nard forgot the hard knocks life had dealt him.

"You know, son, I got boxes up here in the closet of Sticks's clothes and what not. I never knew what to do with them. I've been holding some of this stuff for years. Why don't you take the boxes? I'm sure if you go through them, you'll find some things you can use. It's all kinds of stuff in there. Go on, take it."

Unable to say no, Nard called a hack and took the six boxes home to his mother's house.

The next day, there was another person on his list that he wanted to reach out for, a place in time he needed to visit once again—his other childhood friend, Poncho. There wasn't one night that he didn't think of that fateful evening so long ago that changed his fate, forever.

He could see the long arm stretched around Poncho's head, securing him tightly in a headlock. He could hear Poncho's voice pleading to Nard to take his captor out. The two men had snuck through an open bathroom window, grabbed his man, and were demanding money and cocaine in exchange for Poncho's life.

"Nard, take this nigga. Take him. I know you can, baby boy, take him," Poncho yelled.

"Let him go, let him go. Let him go and I'll let you live," said Nard, meaning every word he spoke, but trying to be calm as he tried to talk Jeremy into letting his man go.

"Nigga, give me what the fuck I came for or both you motherfuckers is gonna die," said Jeremy with lots of heart, pushing the gun harder into the side of Poncho's head as the gun fired a single deadly shot. He looked down at the floor. Lance was dead. *Oh, my God, he killed him, he killed Lance.*

"Motherfucker, I ain't giving you shit. Let him go!" Nard yelled.

"Take him Nard, what the fuck is you waiting fo—"

Poncho's blood and fragments of his head landed all over the wall and covered the entire side of the room. His blood even splattered on Nard, all this within a matter of seconds.

Nard couldn't sleep without waves of memories, silently haunting him every night of his life. He had to visit, if for no other reason than to pay his respects to his man's family. To let them know that he was sorry for what happened to Poncho that night so long ago. And that he tried to do everything in his power to save his life.

The next day off from stocking shelves at ShopRite, he made it a point to cross town and take the Septa bus up to Germantown Avenue where Poncho's family last resided.

Sure enough, he recognized his sister sitting on the porch stoop as he walked up the block.

"Karla-Jae, is that you?"

"Bernard Guess, you're home. How have you been?" she said, hugging Nard as his penis got hard from her body press.

"Yeah, I'm home, Karla-Jae," he said. He had always had a yearning for his man's sister, but never did get with her.

Karla-Jae looked just like she did when they were young.

"Damn, you ain't changed one bit," said Nard, smiling.

"You neither. It's so good to see you. Wait till I tell Liddles," she said, looking up at her brother's friend.

"Damn, you know I must've had a crush on you all my life," she said as she let him go, standing back to take a good look at him. "You look good, you been taking care of yourself," she acknowledged.

"Yeah, that time took a lot from me, though. Shit made my ass gray." He smiled, showing her a few strands he had on the side of his face, next to his ears.

"Awww, that ain't nothing, my whole head is gray, child. I got to color it, every week, damn near," she said, smiling, as she opened her cell phone and dialed her brother's number.

"Wait till he finds out you're here, he's gonna go crazy, watch," she said. Nard couldn't take his eyes off her. And the fact that she had had a crush on him half her life was the ego booster he had needed.

He watched as she spoke into her receiver, smiling her pearly whites and blinking her mascara-brushed eyelashes.

Liddles stopped what he was doing when he heard Nard was over at the house and came straight there. He had always looked up to Nard. He was Poncho's best friend, his closest friend. The way Liddles saw it, Nard was a hero. He had gunned down and killed his brother's assailants. He didn't flinch or give up anything to those bastards. And Liddles knew that if not for Nard's killing them, they would have gotten away and no one would have ever known who took his brother's life.

"Yo, look who it is. It's good to see you, baby," said Liddles, hugging his hero.

"It's good to see you, too," said Nard, all smiles as he and Liddles shook hands, locked in their manly embrace, and stared at one another with their hearts in their eyes.

"You looking real good, homie," said Nard, as he noticed how fresh Liddles's gear was. Liddles was wearing a Loro Piana button-down, a fresh new pair of true religions, and his brand-new air force ones, white on white, of course.

"Yeah, man, you, too."

"Naw, you really looking good. What's that?" asked Nard, looking at Liddles's car.

"That's that Bentley coupe, nigga, sitting on twenty-twos, Ock. Nigga, you know how I do. I get it in, baby. I gets this shit in."

It was the most beautiful car Nard had ever seen. Nard knew then that Liddles was playing with some paper if he was rolling like that in a Bentley coupe, and not ShopRite money either. Shit, Nard could barely catch public transportation with his ShopRite money, so to see his man's little brother ballin' just took his breath away.

Just then Liddles's cell phone went off.

"Hold up, Nard," he said as he answered the phone, conducting his business as usual. He hung up the phone. "Yo, Nard, I got to make this run, and I'm going out of town making a run down to the Carolinas, but I need to hook up with you when I get back. I got something for you, baby boy. I been holding a little something for you, ya heard," Liddles smiled, tapping Nard on the shoulder. "I got a little something for you to help them ends meet, baby," said Liddles, talking his talk.

"Damn, I sure could use it, I just got out the halfway house, and this ShopRite gig I got ain't for shit," said Nard, shaking his head, lost at the perception of how Liddles was moving and shaking.

"ShopRite, fuck ShopRite, you want to work, I'll give you a job. I got a crew. They working on guttin' out this building for me now. You can do that and oversee these motherfuckers, make sure they all doing what they suppose to do, feel me?" asked Liddles in all seriousness.

"Yeah, yeah, you know me, I'm down for whatever," said Nard, figuring it best that he try to get in where he could fit in 'cause at the rate he was going stocking shelves, he'd be assed out if he didn't make some kind of moves. His life had been taken from him, stripped, and he was determined to build it back up. He had dreams, big dreams, and he knew he could make it, despite all the shit he had been through in his life. He just needed a chance, or better yet the right connect, the right hookup, the right little brother of his best friend whose life had been lost along with his twenty years ago.

"Okay, here, take my number and call me. You got a cell?" asked Liddles, writing down his number for Nard.

"Naw, I ain't get one yet, but I'm working on it," said Nard.

"Don't worry, I'll take care of all that for you. What's your shoe size and your dress size?" Liddles asked, playing his part.

Nard gave him everything he asked him for and for the first time he was looking forward to something other than his usual weekly peep shows.

"Don't forget, when I get back, ya heard. I'ma change your whole fucking life," said Liddles as he closed the Bentley's door. He rolled down his window and hollered out to Nard, "Let me find out them white folks got you bagging groceries at fucking ShopRite. Don't worry, I got you." Liddles laughed before racing his engine and driving off down the street.

FBI Building
Fifth and Market Streets
Philadelphia, Pennsylvania

Vivian Lang sat at a tiny coffee table in a small café on the first floor of the federal building where she worked. Time had aged her, but she still looked good. Her makeup wasn't heavy, but you could tell she was wearing it, giving her a more youthful appearance. She looked up at the sight of her ex-husband, Tommy, off in the distance, his arms swinging as if he had not a care in the world.

What in the hell did I ever see in him? And if it wasn't for me, keeping my mouth shut, he never would have made lieutenant. Unfuckingbelievable!

She looked at him as he walked down the hall. Tommy was getting older and more mature, but even after all these years and all the time that had passed, she still despised him. His childish demeanor and lack of responsibility resembled that of a tsetse fly. She remembered the day all hell broke loose, as if it were yesterday. Even though it was almost twenty years ago, the images in her memory still rang clear. Tommy was getting dressed, the baby was screaming, and the babysitter was doing all she could to quell the tiny tot. Vivian had just gotten a call in, another bank robbery, and this time, it was a hostage situation.

"Tommy, I gotta go. Deputy Stevens is going to be looking for me. He said to hightail it and get my ass downtown to Constitution Bank pronto. You don't need anything, do you?" she asked, before kissing him lightly on the cheek and busting out of their bedroom door and down the hall.

"Why's my boy crying?" she asked, picking up Tommy, Jr., as she walked through the house, giving the babysitter detailed instruction on what to do. She had only been with them for three months, but for Vivian the young, carrot-top teenager had turned out to be a lifesaver. "Don't forget, you can still babysit for me Saturday night, right?"

"Yeah, of course, I already told my mom and dad," she said, smiling as if everything was under control.

"Okay, great. The list is on the fridge, as usual. You got my cell phone number if you need me and my office, right?"

"Yes, I have them," Gabby replied as she pulled her sweater over her head and placed it on the dining room chair.

"Thanks so much, you're a lifesaver," said Vivian as she patted Gabby on the back before rushing out the door and hopping into her car. Gabby waved as Vivian reversed out of the driveway. She closed the door behind her and watched Vivian's lights fade away in the distance.

Vivian put on her seatbelt halfway down the block. She tilted her rearview mirror, looked at herself, then tilted her mirror back in place. It was a habit she hadn't broken over the years.

And just as she was about to hop onto I-76 and head downtown she realized she had left the key she needed to unlock the cabinets in her office. *Damn it, I left my file cabinet keys.*

Why didn't I grab them before I left the house, she seethed as she turned down a one-way street behind a trash truck. She looked in her rearview mirror as another car turned down the same street behind her, blocking her in. What could have taken five minutes now took her ten.

By the time she got back to the house she was definitely late and definitely preparing herself to hear Deputy Stevens's mouth when she finally arrived.

"What the fuck?" she gasped, needing air as she opened the door to her bedroom and looked at Tommy, his pants and boxers dangling around his ankles, and in front of him, the babysitter, down on her knees, wearing no shirt, no bra, no socks, just light blue lace panties. He didn't even see her standing in the doorway of their bedroom.

Unable to move, she stood still and calm, watching and wondering what it was she should do. Calmly, she closed the door behind her. She breathed a deep and heavy sigh, tears beginning to stream down her face. She could hear Gabby moaning now, their mattress squeaking from movement. *He's fucking her? Great, he's fucking her, like right now in my bed... at that.*

Vivian quietly made it down the stairs as the sounds of Gabby getting pounded by her husband got louder and louder with every step. She grabbed the knob to the front door of their home but she couldn't turn it, she couldn't leave, she froze as she flashed through her mind her life as she knew it with Tommy. It was a life that would be no more. *How could he? She's the babysitter, she's in our home. What the hell is wrong with him?* She couldn't believe he would stoop so low. *She's a little kid, for Pete's sake.* The thought of him sleeping with a girl only fifteen left her hollow. The thought of him sleeping with her in her bed disgusted her. Vivian was incredibly angry, but she didn't want to show it. She had learned to stay calm and never let them see you sweat, never show your true face. Vivian ran back up the stairs and, as if it was nothing, barged into her bedroom and stormed over to her closet as Tommy continued fucking Gabby doggie style, not realizing the vision of his wife was reality.

"Vivian, what the fuck!" he yelled, pulling his dick out of Gabby, exposing both himself and her to Vivian.

"Oh, I'm sorry, did I distract you from fucking our fifteen-year-old babysitter?"

"Vivian, I'm sorry," said Tommy, grabbing part of the blanket to cover his lower body. Gabby was behind him, using him for cover as she covered her naked body with Vivian's sheets.

"Aren't you twelve? Do your parents know what you're doing, little girl, fucking a forty-year-old married man with a child in the other room that you're supposed to be babysitting?"

"I'm turning sixteen next week," Gabby began before Vivian

attacked her, smacking her in the face, pulling her hair, yelling and screaming for her to get out of her house.

"Vivian, stop, what the fuck is wrong with you," said Tommy as he pulled Vivian off Gabby.

"Get off me," said Vivian, struggling with Tommy. "You fucking piece of shit, I fucking hate you," she screamed, and of course by now, Gabby had grabbed her things and was hightailing it down the stairs.

"You little fucking whore," said Vivian as she threw the girl's shoes down the flight of stairs, trying to hit her in the head with them, missing her by the hair on a toad's ass as the shoes slammed into the front door.

"Please, Vivian, I'm sorry," said Tommy, never in a million years having thought that he'd ever get caught.

"You fucking disgust me. I will never trust you, in our house, in our bed. I swear to God, I fucking hate you. I want a divorce!"

It was twenty years later, and nothing had changed. She still despised him, and he despised her for all the shit she had done to hurt him over the years. Twenty years later and here they were, still hating.

"Yeah, so what's this about?" he asked as he approached the table. "Shit, better be good, too," he added, not wanting to be bothered with her at all.

"I tried to tell you, just sign the papers," she said, pointing to admission forms for their son's entrance to college.

"I'm not signing shit," said Tommy, refusing the papers as he pushed them back at her.

"They're for college for Tommy, Jr., Tommy. Stop being such a fucking asshole and sign them," she said, shoving them back in his face.

"I'm an asshole, I'm an asshole? Are you fucking kidding me?

You're the fucking asshole. Where the fuck is my brother, Vivian?"

"Don't ask me that!" she said, not wanting to hear it for the ninety-ninth time.

"No, where is he? All because I fucked our babysitter, you fucking put my brother in jail?"

"Tommy, he was robbing banks, he shot at the police, he would have been caught anyway. At least I helped him."

"You fucking helped him all right, you helped him go to jail."

"Fuck you, you were so busy fucking cheating on me with our fucking babysitter," spat Vivian, wanting to choke the life out of him.

"So what, so what?" he said.

"So what, she was our fifteen-year-old babysitter, you asshole. You fucking cheat on me with a fifteen-year-old, then turn around and marry her, and you're mad about Sammy? I did my job. Now do yours and pretend you're a father and sign the fucking papers so I don't have to take you back to court again."

"Fuck you," said Tommy, hating everything about Vivian. "I don't know how I ever loved you. How did I even fuck you?" he spat at her, trying to figure out what the fuck he had been thinking. The entire time they had been together, she silently had him under investigation. She had all the proof the department needed to implicate Tommy Delgado in a number of felonies. And she always made it perfectly clear that if anything were ever to happen to her, he could kiss his sweet ass good-bye.

"Umm, let me see, you put your penis in my vagina and humped really fast. Fuck you, I should have arrested you along with your brother for fucking a minor, not to mention the rest of your criminally insane family."

"Yeah, you ain't that fucking stupid. You know what the fuck my criminally insane family would do to you. You fucking know, don't ya, Viv?" He smiled at her, wanting to fucking choke her like a bird, just as her phone rang.

"I'm on my way, I'll be right there." She hung up and looked at Tommy. "I have work to do. I have to go. You signing for Tommy, Jr., or do I have to contact Uncle Carmen and get him to get you to sign?" she asked, smiling as if she didn't care what it would take. She and Carmen had always remained close; he still made her his famous chicken a la Rocco sandwich.

"You're a cunt. I swear to God, I just want to..." he said signing the papers as she stood above him, waiting for her paperwork back.

"Want to what, Lieutenant?" she dared him. "You'll fucking do nothing to me, and you fucking know it. You'll go home and you'll keep pretending, that's what you'll do," she said as she bent down and whispered in his ear, threatening him with a life in prison if something happened to her. "Don't even think about anything happening to me or I will fuck you like you never been fucked before. You got that, asshole?"

"You're a fucking cunt," said Tommy, knowing that Vivian's FBI ass could take him and his family down in a blink of an eye, but she never would, for the sake of Tommy, Jr.

"And you're an asshole," she added, snatching the paperwork he had finally signed from him. "I don't know what I ever saw in you, fucking idiot," she mumbled as she walked away.

"I don't know what I ever saw in you, fucking bitch!" mumbled Tommy, thinking of how she had ruined his life.

"True, so true." Vivian smiled as she sashayed out of the café and down the hall.

Nard made it home from work the next night a little early. The six boxes he had gotten from Ms. Kay were still stacked in his room. He felt good to have finally found some real-life memories from his past. He was anxious to see his charitable donations from Sticks's mother and what Sticks had in the boxes. With his luck he might find at least a sweater or maybe even a jacket he could wear. Little did he know, he would find much more than that.

He went through the box of clothes, holding up shirts and pants, remembering his old friend. He thought of that night so long ago. How they had killed Poncho and almost killed him. That night surely changed the rest of his life; that night was a night he would never forget as long as he lived. As far as he was concerned, Lance Robertson and Jeremy Tyler got exactly what they deserved. And he should have never had to serve one day in prison for murdering them. *If I hadn't killed them, they would have killed me, for sure. I did what I had to do, what anybody would have done.*

A taped-up sneaker box was hidden under a sweater. Nard anxiously removed the tape, opened the box, and revealed scattered photos and several VCR tapes.

What we got here? Nard asked his growing penis. *Oh, my God, I remember this.*

"Yo, Sticks, I swear on my moms. Oh, my God!" an overly excited Nard jumped up and circled the room, talking to his dead friend.

"You okay?" asked Beverly, peeking in the door of the room where Nard had taken up residence.

"Oh, yeah, I'm good," said Nard as he stopped himself from pacing, stood still, faced his mother, and calmed himself, folding his hands in front of him.

"It's a lot of noise coming from in there, jumping around and what-not," said Beverly, shaking her head and making her way downstairs to where her uncle was sitting watching *Jeopardy*.

"What's all that noise; sounds like a kangaroo jumping around," said Uncle Ray Ray, looking at her over the top of his bifocals.

"I don't know, but there's something wrong with Nard. I feel like we need to do something to get him some help."

"Ain't no help for him, just leave him alone," said Uncle Ray Ray before busting out in a Michael Jackson verse and singing to his niece.

"I'ma leave you alone all right, leave you right in here by yourself," she said, getting up and going in the kitchen.

Upstairs, Nard was going at it, stroking his dick as he sifted through picture after picture. This was actually just as good as the XXX store he went to. Sticks's pictures were as graphic as graphic could get. He laid the top photo down, revealing the next. It was like a freeze flash from a moment in time. His hand slowly moved from his penis to the photo as he took it from one hand to the other and held it under the light. *That's that bitch right there.* He saw her face, clear as day, just as he remembered in the courtroom. The photo was from the night Sticks's man was having a bachelor party. Nard didn't attend but he knew the groom and most of the others. Sticks and the guys planned on celebrating and needed some strippers, because what was a bachelor party without strippers? He called Daisy, a stripper from the Honey Dipper, a strip club he frequented. Sticks got her and her friend Trixie and took them to a hotel. He put them in a room and told them to order what they wanted to eat and brought them a bottle of champagne. Unknown to them, the champagne was spiked, and after some chicken wings and three glasses of champagne, they lost their motor skills and their bodies became limp. While aware of their surroundings, both girls were unable to function. Daisy had impaired sight and was unable to lift her arms, stand, or walk. She knew she wanted to say "no" or "stop" but was barely able to speak, letting out a soft whisper, raising her arms in protest, but unable to hold them up, and unable to resist being bound and held down. But she could hear clearly. Daisy and Trixie had sex with God knows how many different men that night and it was all caught on video. That night was right there in the palm of Nard's hands in living color. Not only did Sticks take photographs, he videotaped the whole thing. Nard quickly popped the VCR tape into the VCR machine, turned on his television, and pressed play. He locked the bedroom door and sat on the edge of the bed, his manhood growing as he grabbed the shaft of his penis and began moving his hand slowly up and down as he watched Daisy giving fellatio to one guy while another hit her in the ass. She looked as if she wanted it. She wasn't screaming or crying, she was taking it like it was nothing.

This fucking whore could fuck these niggas like this, but she couldn't say I was with her. I wish I was there that night, I would've fucked this bitch and busted her fucking ass. Nard stroked himself, squeezing a little tighter around his dick as his hand guided itself faster and faster until he came, his semen shooting everywhere.

Nard fantasized so much about fucking Daisy he had to catch himself constantly. Just thoughts of fucking her, for payback if for nothing else, made him explode. His sexual thoughts were one thing, but deep down, he hated Daisy. He wished nothing more than for all the pain he had suffered to be passed on to her. She had ruined his life. It was because of her he went to jail in the first place. He got jammed all because of her. Had she come through, it would never have gone down the way it did. But in the end,

Nard would see to it that she'd pay with her life, one way or the other.

I wonder where this bitch is at? She's out there somewhere, but where? I got to track this bitch down, got to, if it's the last thing I ever do.

A GANGSTER'S REUNION

The next week, one night after Nard got off work he called Liddles.

"I been getting everything ready for you all day, man, where you been? You got me sitting here taking every call that come through," he said jokingly.

"What you getting ready for me?" Nard asked, feeling real special.

"Yo, I got you, I told you last week."

And Liddles did. He rounded up everybody he knew that Nard knew, everybody from back in the day that rolled with his brother, Poncho. All those still out in the streets that they kicked it with, and he invited them to Ruth Chris. The bill would be on him tonight and just as dinner was complete, a brand new Cadillac Escalade, snowball white with black interior, pulled up and parked outside the restaurant on Broad Street in downtown Philly.

It was a night to remember. Nard mingled with folks he hadn't seen in over twenty years. How Liddles managed to round everybody up, he didn't have a clue. And Liddles pulled out all the stops, making sure he was treated like a king. And when dinner was complete, the dinner party made its way outside to watch

Liddles give Nard his brand-new truck.

"Yo, Nard," said Liddles, throwing him the key to the Escalade.

"What's this?" asked Nard, rolling the funny-looking black object around in his hand.

"It's the key to your truck, nigga," said Liddles, smiling.

Nard looked at the Escalade, unbelieving.

"What, you looking like you forgot how to drive," joked Liddles.

"Shit, this motherfucker so pretty," he said, slapping fives with Liddles, "I'm scared to get behind the wheel." Looking at the car, just the thought of it, had him under pressure.

"Don't worry, I'm rocking with you, I'll drive," said Liddles, taking the key from him and ordering him to get in.

"Umm, Nard, excuse me," said a soft voice behind a sweet smile.

"Hey, Lisa, thanks for coming out," said Nard.

"Oh, I wouldn't miss seeing you for the world," she said. "Here, take my number, call me any time, okay?" She smiled as she passed the number to him.

Nard smiled back, his dick harder than it had ever been.

"Yeah, I'll call you tomorrow."

"Okay, maybe we can get together for dinner or drinks or something," she said, happy to have made contact with her long lost daydream.

"Come on, playboy, you got time for all that," said Liddles, breaking their moment.

Shit, no I don't, thought Nard, following behind Liddles, wondering if Lisa was as soft as she looked.

Liddles hopped in the driver's seat as Nard rode shotgun. He went down to the water at Piers Landing and parked the Escalade in a vacant parking lot.

The two men sat talking for hours. Nard listened to everything Liddles told him, taking him back twenty years ago all the way to his trial, when he had his sister Karla-Jae wearing wigs and reporting back to him as he sat outside the courthouse in a beat-up, dusty van. He told Nard how he had followed Wink, and the other families. How he gunned them all down, and how Wink had pleaded for his life. How the police had questioned him, had a statewide manhunt for the murderer, but couldn't tie him in, and never made an arrest. Nard sat and listened to every word.

"I swear on my moms, I ain't never told nobody this shit," said Liddles as he continued. "See, the nigga, Wink, said he had fifty thousand in the basement. But I was there on some murder shit, know what I mean, and I killed him. But that fifty rang in my head all night. So, bong, the next day I went back to their block and I waited out there with the neighborhood, like an innocent bystander, and after all the police was gone and the neighborhood was quiet and the house was empty, I bought a flashlight from the corner store, broke into the house through the basement window, and don't you know, this nigga really did have two trash bags filled with ones and fives. I swear to God, he had fifty thousand in two trash bags right next to some boxes. This was the thing, though, I had to go back out the window, 'cause I didn't want to get caught going out the front door and I ain't have nothing to put the money in."

"What did you do?" asked Nard, really into the story.

"Went back out the fucking window." He laughed, slapping high fives with Nard. "I took the two trash bags and threw them on my back, baby, and walked down the street with my nine in my hoodie so if I had to pop the fuck off, I'd be ready, and I got in my car, fifty thousand dollars richer. You know, Poncho had a stash in our moms house, and she gave everybody a little piece, but that wasn't nothing. Once I got that fifty out that basement, I went to Simon Shuller and the nigga put me on."

"He used to look out for me when I was in jail. He always sent packages and money for my books. I been trying to get at him, you know where he at?"

"Yeah, I think they gave Dizzy like forty years. He's upstate running the shit out of Graterford, and Simon he's been dead now, what, about five years?"

"Wow, Simon's dead?"

"Yeah, man, this game's crazy, here today, gone tomorrow," said Liddles, thinking about the years, time, and how it traveled.

"I need to get at Dizzy bad," said Nard.

"Go on up to Graterford, all you need is your ID."

"Damn," said Nard, "life is really crazy, but if I had known this shit, I'da found you a lot sooner."

"Been waiting for you, Nard, I been waiting for you."

"So, that's how you came up?"

"Yup, that nigga was pleading for his life and really had all that fucking money in the basement."

"Wow," said Nard, "that's unbelievable."

"Yeah, that was my come up, that dead nigga's spare change, his ones and his fives, in his momma's basement."

"Good thing you went back."

"Yeah, it was a good thing, even though it couldn't bring back Poncho, you know."

"Yeah, I know."

"But you killed those bastards trying to save Ponch's life. You killed them and I been holding this for you waiting for you to come home," said Liddles, sliding Nard a briefcase. He took one look inside at the stacks of money.

"What's this?"

"It's for you, man, I flipped and put your fifty to the side. I've been holding that for you, waiting for you to come home."

Nard looked at the money. He couldn't believe Poncho's little brother.

"Damn, I really would have been here a lot sooner, if I knew you had all this for me." Nard smiled, full of zest and glee. He didn't know what to say. He was frozen. This was the most that anyone besides his mother had done for him in his whole entire forty-two years of life. He looked at Liddles, his man's little brother. He now felt that his time was well served, if for nothing else, for Poncho.

The two sat for hours and talked shop. Liddles had his hands in all kinds of pies, some that baked legally and others that baked illegally. At the end of the day they all baked the same, fruitfully. On the strength of his brother, and some real-life gangster shit, Liddles had not only passed Nard a suitcase full of money, but the key to the city along with it.

Graterford Prison, Graterford, Pennsylvania
Two Weeks Later

It took Liddles a minute to get Dizzy's government, but once he got it, he passed the information to Nard, who was rolling through the city with his top down screaming money at a thing.

He went through the rigorous security checkpoint and sat down at the assigned visiting room table.

It was then that he saw an old man walk through the door to the visiting room and make his way slowly over to the table. Dizzy had aged tremendously over the past ten years behind bars. The thought of dying in prison wasn't a happy one, but it was inevitable.

"How you doing," said Nard, standing and extending his hand.

"Well, I guess I'm doing as good as I'm going to in this rat trap they got me in," said Dizzy.

"Thanks for seeing me," said Nard.

"You entitled," spat back Dizzy, letting him know that even at eighty-three he still had his street swagger.

The two men talked and Dizzy soon realized that all Nard's small talk and beating around the bush led to one thing, a series of questions that could give him what he needed, and what he needed was answers and closure.

"Who killed Sticks?" asked Nard, wanting to know what happened.

Dizzy sat still and quiet for a moment, thinking of whether he should speak on the matter. He remembered everything like it was yesterday.

"I was locked up, I knew nothing. I stuck to my guns and next thing I knew, the girl was on the stand saying she never saw me in her life. That bitch ruined my life, man, ruined my shit, for real."

It was then that Dizzy understood where Nard was coming from, and it was then that he decided to give him what he came for…knowledge.

"See, Sticks was running around in them streets and he was like a loose cannon. Every time we turned around he had another body, another mess, and Simon never liked messes. So, when he killed the girl's landlord, that was the final straw, you understand. And Simon made the call, he sent a hitter down to Nashville with Sticks with the orders to bring back the girl, and leave Sticks behind."

Nard lowered his head as he sat and listened to Dizzy tell him that it was his own team that turned on him.

"I'm not sure what went wrong, but the cops brought back the girl, Sticks and the hitter were both killed, and the girl didn't testify like she was supposed to. That's all I know."

"What happened to her, where did she go?"

"Oh, the police took the girl into protective custody, and of course you got sentenced, and Simon felt so bad, you know we did everything for you, everything, after you went to jail."

"I appreciate it, too, 'cause they had me fucked up in Green. If it hadn't been for those packages, I don't know what I would have done."

The two men sat for a moment as Nard registered the story that Dizzy was unfolding.

"You said Nashville?" questioned Nard.

"Yeah, when Sticks got hold of the girl's landlord, he was the one that gave up the girl, said she had family down in Nashville."

That was it. That was all he needed to start his search for Daisy Mae Fothergill and her family in Nashville, Tennessee.

He sat with Dizzy for the afternoon and talked. They talked about the mix-up, how Nard was supposed to go to Graterford, but was shipped to Green inadvertently, and how the message to protect the young man went to the wrong facility. That explained the second mishap, which had caused Nard's sentence to be altered from one to twenty.

After a long afternoon, Nard had more answers to a life he hadn't lived than a person who had. Dizzy was one of the coolest old heads he'd ever have the pleasure of spending an afternoon with. He definitely knew his shit, and he definitely knew the streets. He wasn't missing a beat either, and the fact that he was spending the rest of his life in prison didn't stop his roll. He was doing the same thing he did in the street, he was just doing it behind bars.

After an afternoon of conversation, Nard rose, ready to go. He had gotten all that he needed and then some. And thanks to Liddles's breaking him off, he had the finances to track down Daisy. Thanks to Dizzy, he had a direction to begin with. It would only be a matter of time, and vengeance would be his, and so would Daisy's ass.

FREEZE

Early one morning, just as the sun was rising, the FBI stationed themselves on Daniel Boone's front lawn. Through a long series of investigations over the past twenty years and video enhancement, the FBI had finally cracked the code on the abandoned baby cases from 1986.

Vivian and her team positioned themselves as she rang the doorbell.

As soon as Boone opened the door, Vivian flashed her badge and announced herself.

"I'm Special Agent Vivian Lang; are you Mr. Daniel Adam Boone?"

"Um... yeah... what's this all about?"

He asked the question as if he had no clue why a special agent for the FBI could possibly be standing on his front porch. He was, after all, a law-abiding citizen, if ever there was one.

"I'm investigating several abandoned baby cases from the late eighties to early nineties and I was wondering if I could ask you a couple of questions? May I come in?" she said, moving closer to the door.

Daniel Boone looked as if he had seen a ghost. His skin turned pale white, his pupils dilated, and a bead of sweat rolled down the side of his face.

"Mr. Boone, do you mind if I come in?" asked Vivian again, standing at the door toe to toe with him, waiting for a response.

Without warning or hesitation, Daniel Boone used all his strength and shoved Vivian's chest so hard that she fell backward against one of the porch beams. She lunged toward him, but Daniel slammed the door with all his might as Vivian's shoulder took the impact. He was running through the house when she crashed through the wooden door, dislocating her shoulder, but pursuing Boone all the same.

"Freeze," she shouted, popping off two rounds at Daniel's back as he dipped into the kitchen, grabbing a steak knife and running toward the basement staircase where he planned to kill her. Daniel ran though his house, Vivian and the other FBI agents right behind him screaming "FBI, freeze!" and a bunch of other orders Daniel Boone paid no attention to. He reached the staircase, and was almost to the top when he felt his leg being pulled from behind, causing him to loose his balance. He tripped, tumbling backward into Vivian as they both fell back down the flight of stairs.

"Please, please, please don't hurt me," Daniel Boone screamed as Vivian pounced on him at the bottom of the staircase. She placed him in a headlock.

"I didn't do nothing, it was the doctor. Please, you got to believe me. I didn't do nothing to them babies. I just did like Dr. Vistane told me to. Please, don't send me to jail."

"I can't believe you made me break my god damn nail," said Vivian, slapping the shit out of him and roughing the frail older man up a bit.

"Please, you're hurting me," he said as Vivian pulled out handcuffs and held his hands tightly behind his back.

"Shut up. You are under arrest for kidnapping and child endangerment. You have the right to remain silent. Anything you say can and will be used against you in a court of law. You have the right to an attorney. If you cannot afford one, one will be appointed for you."

"Please, I swear, it wasn't me, it wasn't. It was the doctor, Dr. Vistane, he's crazy, you know. He made me do it, he made me do it," the man said as he began to sob. "I never wanted to leave them. I never wanted to leave them. It's haunted me all my life, all my life. Please don't put me in jail. Please, somebody help me," Vivian watched the man break down in front of her, crying and sobbing uncontrollably. "Help me!"

"Shut up!" she said as she threw him to the floor, his hands handcuffed behind him, and finished reading him his rights.

"Please, ma'am, it wasn't me, it was the doctor," he cried over and over again.

Her backup team was on the scene in a matter of seconds. The local boys were always somewhere nearby, too, when she needed them. They assisted Vivian with the arrest and had the man placed in the back of a paddy wagon where he would be transported to the FBI building for questioning. As with any arrest, news leaked immediately and a team of reporters was on the scene.

"Excuse me, Special Agent Lang, the abandoned church baby case is twenty years old, how did the FBI finally crack the case to make an arrest?"

"Who is the doctor?"

"Do you know where the babies came from or who their parents are?"

A hundred and one questions were thrown at Vivian, and she calmly replied.

"We believe the suspect abandoned the babies on the steps of Catholic churches from 1982 to 1992, and we have taken him into custody for questioning. That's all I can tell you at this time."

The mob of reporters wouldn't settle for that and bombarded her with more questions. Of course, with their assistance, this would become one of the biggest news stories in the history of Philadelphia, and Vivian would be at the forefront of the investigation as the arresting officer.

"She held up her hands, shrugged a "Sorry, Charlie," smiled for the cameras, and waved at the tuned-in audience.

"Jesus fucking Christ, what the fuck, they got this bitch on every fucking channel," yelled Tommy, using the remote to turn the television off before throwing it on the sofa.

"Tommy, calm down, you'll give yourself a heart attack," said Gabby, rubbing his back, trying to calm him down. "You always get yourself upset with her."

"I fucking hate her, she's the biggest bitch in the world, the entire fucking world," he said, jealous and pissed that she was getting the glory for solving a case and he wasn't.

Two Months Later

Nard pulled his Escalade up to the sidewalk and threw it in park. He hopped out of the car. It was Thanksgiving and almost a year since he'd been home. He looked at the writing on a tiny piece of paper he held in his hand. It held the initials KSW and an address in Murfreesboro, Tennessee.

"Hey, ma," he said kissing his mom's cheek as he walked past her sitting on the porch.

"Hey, them people called, left you a number in there on the counter so you can call them back."

"Where's Uncle Ray Ray?"

"He's upstairs lying down. I don't think he was feeling too good today. He said he was tired," said Beverly.

Nard ran upstairs, grabbed a bag that he had packed the night before, and ran back down the stairs.

"Where are you going?" Beverly asked, confused and concerned at the sight of the overnight bag.

He had no response, and stopped in his tracks to think of one. "I got to go out of town and take care of something."

And he did. It turned out the same private investigator who was hired on his behalf to get a statement from Daisy had been hired by Simon Shuller, and Dizzy was able to give Nard the contact. When Daisy met with private investigator to give the alibi statement for Nard and collect her two thousand dollars, she had completed an intake sheet, and she listed her mother, Abigail Wright, as her next of kin. That same investigator tracked down the entire family and her closest living relative, her cousin, Kimmie Sue, still living in Murfreesboro, Tennessee. Once Nard was informed of his findings, he immediately stopped what he was doing, went home, and began to pack his bags.

"You going out of town to take care of something?" asked Beverly, looking at her son as if she knew better. "Take care of what, like you some traveling salesman? Them parole people know you going out of town?"

Nard didn't answer her, and his silence told her what she would have to do, should they come around while he was gone…LIE. And of course she would, because she would do anything to keep him safe and keep them from locking up her baby. Nard passed her a plastic bag wrapped tightly with rubber bands.

He didn't say a word, simply looking piercingly at Beverly, letting her know he wasn't playing games. Inside the plastic bag he passed to his moms was forty thousand dollars.

"What's this?" she asked, and he again ignored her question.

"Take that," said Nard, watching his mother gasp at the contents of the plastic bag. "Hold that, just in case you need something."

"Oh, my God, boy, what the hell you done did? Nard, you robbed a bank? What, you selling drugs again?" she asked with her "what the hell" expression still on her face.

"No, Mom, I ain't selling drugs again," said Nard, and while he wasn't at the present time, he did have real big triple-beam plans in his future alongside Liddles.

"Well, where is you going then? And where'd all this money come from?"

Nard put his arms around her as if he was only five and hugged her.

"I love you, Mom."

"I love you too, son."

He let her go and Beverly watched as Nard walked out the door, never answering her questions, never speaking of where he was going or when he'd return.

"Please don't let nothing bad happen to him," she whispered to God, as the porch door closed behind him and he faded down the steps.

Just as Nard turned the corner of the block, Beverly heard her best friend for the past fifty years knocking at the door.

"What in the hell is Maeleen doing?" asked Donna, as Beverly opened the door. Donna pointed across the street to Maeleen.

The two women stood quietly as they watched Maeleen lighting candles that she had placed in a long row on the sidewalk in front of her house.

"What is she doing?" asked Beverly, squinting and wishing she had her glasses.

"Who the hell knows, you're her neighbor. Shit, she's probably over there lighting her candles so she can chant it up with the Moonlight God," Donna joked.

"I think you're right," said Beverly as the two women went inside, falling out with laughter as they closed the door behind them so Maeleen wouldn't hear them.

DEATH BECOMES HER

One Week Later

It was a rainy Tuesday as the funeral home prepared for the services for Kimberly Sue Wright. Nard looked on as if he were her closest friend or a friend of the family. He took a seat in the back of the church, sitting in the third row from the last row of pews, watching and waiting. He was quiet and reserved, dressed in a dark black suit, and extremely well groomed. He looked nothing out of the ordinary and when approached was calm and collected.

"Kimmie"—he had learned her nickname by reading the pamphlet being passed out that was on display as you entered the church—had lived a full life.

"She was a very dear friend to me, always there when I needed someone to lean on, always a kind spirit to me, and she is someone that I will miss dearly," he said as he looked down at her lifeless body.

"She was a friend to many," said a stranger, patting him on the back.

He looked so dashing, so debonair, that his presence suggested he was a previous suitor in her life and had come to say goodbye. Kimmie was a beautiful woman, even in death. Nard looked at her body lying in the casket in the front of the church. He couldn't escape thoughts of killing her as he stared at her cold, dead body. He desperately wanted to project a look of sadness, of a broken man, maybe an old boyfriend, so he tried to think sad thoughts, but he couldn't. All he could think of was climbing into her bedroom window and waiting in the closet for her to come home, as any other normal intruder would. He was wearing a black ski-mask, with gloves on his hands and shoe mitts covering his Tims. The rope in his pants pocket, long enough to strangle her, was all it would take.

Kimberly came home from work on time as usual. He could hear her entering the apartment from the bedroom closet he was hiding in. He looked at his watch. *Same time as the past three days,* he thought to himself. *At least she's punctual, if nothing else.* Nard heard the locks turning and the door to her apartment opening as he pulled the rope from his pocket, making sure it was there before stuffing it back. He patiently waited, and waited, and waited, resting patiently on a plastic bag of clothes that was in the corner of the closet.

Kimmie, home from work after a long hard day, did her normal routine. She played with her cat, Mittens, for a few minutes, stroking him and rubbing him behind his ears, and then she opened a can of his favorite food and served him his dinner. Then she poured a glass of white wine and made her dinner, eating it on a tray in front of her living room television, drinking another glass of wine afterward, taking a shower, and finally, lights out.

He made sure she had had enough time to fall quietly to sleep, then tiptoed from the bedroom closet over to the side of her bed, making sure not to make a sound. He stood over her, looking at her body under the sheets. She was resting peacefully, and he decided not to choke her, but to suffocate her. He lifted a pillow lying next to her as she opened her eyes.

"Who are you?" she asked, as if in a dream, but realizing she wasn't, she began to scream.

Nard quickly took the pillow and covered her face. Kimberly fought off her attacker as best she could, but her fight was useless. Moments later, her body went limp as the last breath of air escaped her and Nard suffocated her to death.

Like a thief in the night, he left and waited patiently for her body to be discovered, her family to be notified, and her next of kin to come claim her. It was impossible to track down a person in police protective custody. Instead, Nard had decided to go about it another way, and what better way than this? The only question was whether it would work. And of course it did. Nard spotted Daisy the moment she walked through the door. His heart pounded as she walked by. This was the woman that had ruined his life. Sure, she had aged, but her face was the same, her eyes unforgettable, and besides maybe an added ten pounds, she looked just like the girl in the video he had become used to masturbating to every night. *You fucking sold me out, bitch, you fucking hung me. We'll see now, though, we'll see now.* She was dressed all in black, carrying a black clutch in her hand, a black clutch that before the day was out would be missing, until it was found in the bathroom of the funeral home.

"See, you probably left it. You've been so upset, this has been a very trying week," said Webster, rubbing his wife's back as he consoled her.

"You're right, it has been quite stressful. I just can't believe she's gone. Now I have no one."

"Yes, but at least you have your bag, and you have me," he said, trying to cheer her up. "The most important thing is that you took care of everything for your cousin. You gave her a wonderful homecoming. And yes, the stress of leaving your bag is nothing, we found it, and all is well. Now, I'd say it's time to catch our flight back to Scottsdale."

Nard watched as the suited gentleman escorted Daisy, as if she couldn't walk on her own, out the door and into a rented 760 Volvo.

"I'll see y'all back in Scottsdale," Nard said as he nodded to himself, looking at the address he had written down from her driver's license. "Yep, looks like I'll be seeing both y'all motherfuckers in a minute."

THE COME BACK

Scottsdale, Arizona
One Month Later

Diana Praeliou emerged from the kitchen patio. "It's absolutely beautiful out today," she said to her husband as he kissed her cheek. "A perfect day for a hot-air balloon ride," she said, like a kid wanting a lollipop in a candy store.

"I wish I could, but you know I'm out of here today."

"Oh, yeah, that," she said, having completely forgotten. "I remember, you did say that you had a convention in Miami, and next month, the Doctrine of Medical Excellence Ceremony, which I'm shopping for a dress to wear to as we speak."

"I know my schedule is tight."

"You think?" she asked sarcastically. "Do you think you could pencil me in for a quiet dinner alone, just the two of us?"

"Someone has to pay the bills around here, Diana."

"This is true, and you do a wonderful job, honey," she said jokingly, wrapping her arms around him.

"Do you remember the first time I ever hugged you?" he asked, as he lovingly stared into his wife's eyes.

The first time we hugged. Only he would remember the first time we hugged. Jeez, he always does this to me.

"Hmmm, now let me see, darling," she said, playing for more time.

"You don't remember, so I might as well tell you."

"No, I do, I do, wait," she said, as her husband began fidgeting and tickling her sides.

"I know, stop that, our first hug, body to body, was at the game. Remember, the Hawks won the game seven to zero, remember, and I was there cheering and you were watching from the bleachers and you ran down on the field and you hugged me, swung me around, and squeezed the living daylights out of me," she said, batting her perfectly fitted eyelashes at him as she felt his hand sliding down her back and into the middle of her legs.

"Now," she said, as she passionately kissed him.

"Now," he said, as he lay down on top of her, simply destroying her first attempt at getting dressed for the day. They passionately made love as they did most mornings, a perfect start to every waking day they spent together. Webster came inside his wife, taking less than five minutes from start to finish, but leaving Diana with a feeling that could last an eternity.

"I wish you didn't have to go," she said, smiling as she wrapped her arms around her husband and moved her leg in between his, holding on to him as if to let him go would be to let go of her last breath.

"I wish I didn't have to go, too, but can you wait for Spain or what?" he asked, kissing the tip of her nose.

"No, no, I absolutely can't. Spain is going to simply be the best, our fourteenth wedding anniversary, and we're going to see the bullfighting. Oh, my God, Webster, can you believe it's been fourteen years?" she asked.

"No, it doesn't seem like we've been married that long."

"I know, right, but it's been the best ride of my life and you've been the best husband a girl could ask for. I do dreadfully adore you, and I am most proud of you," she said before kissing his lips gently.

"I love you, too, more than you will ever know."

He kissed her cheek as several knocks on their bedroom door startled them.

"Yes, Rosa?" she asked, as Webster walked into the bathroom and out of sight.

"Excuse me, Señora Praeliou, would you like me to make your breakfast now?" asked Rosa, her housekeeper.

"No, I think I'll take a ride this morning. I would like a hot bath drawn for me when I come back and then I'll have my breakfast," she said, tying her hair in a long ponytail on top of her head.

"You going for a ride?"

"Yes. I will see you when you get back. Safe travels, my love," she said, offering a quick peck of the lips to seal the deal of his safely returning to her. While Webster showered, she quickly dressed and grabbed a pair of rusty brown Valentino riding boots from her closet.

The stables where her champion stallion Thoroughbreds were kept was a half-mile walk from the house. Carlos, their butler, had a golf cart. Rosa used a walkie-talkie to reach him, and he was at the side door waiting to whisk Diana away to the stables. Polo, Misfit, and Rags were all retired now from racing, but they had made their owner, Diana Praeliou, a very rich woman. Misfit had won the Kentucky Derby and had taken the Triple Crown. Misfit had made Diana rich beyond her wildest dreams. Rags had won four Grade One races, including the Breeder's Cup Classic at Belmont Park, and he had been Horse of the Year in 2004, 2005, and 2006. He retired with a record of twelve wins, nine second-place finishes, and one third-place finish. His career earnings topped five million four hundred fifty-three thousand dollars, no cents required. She herself would have never believed it had she not known better. Polo, until he injured his left leg, had been a prize-winning racehorse. His record far outweighed that of Misfit and Rags. He took home first place at every race, and every horse show, but after he fell and suffered a fractured leg, she never raced him again. Instead, he retired to a quiet, tranquil life with her. "We might be a little broken, hey, Polo, but we're survivors, huh, boy," she'd always tell him, feeling most attached to him and most grateful for all the high times he had brought her.

It was Webster who first introduced Diana to the thrill of riding. Until then, the last creature she ever dreamed of having for a pet was a horse, but Diana loved her stallions so passionately that she cared for them personally. Even though she had stableboys to walk them, feed them, and brush them daily, she still every day was hands-on with them. For her, they were the babies she never had, and she loved each of them dearly. Some women get dogs from their husbands; Diana got Thoroughbreds. Sometimes she thought she was closer to her horses than she was to her husband. All the time he spent at the hospital and at Bio One's pharmaceutical facility, took up the time he would have spent being the perfect doting husband. But Diana understood, and she gave her husband all the mental and physical support he needed to be one of the creative, genius forces behind Bio One's search for a cure to Alzheimer's. It was unbelievable, and she would have never imagined twenty years ago that her life would be this rich in luxury or love, but it was, and now her husband was receiving recognition for his contributions in medicine. His discoveries were ground-breaking. The practice of medicine had led Webster all over the world to care for the sick. And over the years he had grown into the security of having a beautiful, strong, faithful wife by his side. Not only was Diana the epitome of grace and charm, but she had a feminine quality that other women seemingly could not project. She walked into a room and effortlessly illuminated it. People were attracted to her beauty and charm, and of course most of the men in their tight-knit circle of friends secretly lusted to share her bed. They were unable to take their eyes off her, even in the presence of her husband. If he hadn't been told what a lucky man he was at least one hundred thousand times, his name wasn't Webster Praeliou. Her every move was watched, from how she held her husband's hand, to how she danced the waltz, to every bite she'd take of her liver pâte. And she commanded respect. Had she wished for others to bow as if in the presence of true royalty, then it would have been so. In the secret society of Scottsdale's Who's Who, Webster and Diana Praeliou were at the top of the list, invited to every event and envied by everyone who had the pleasure of being in their company. They were the social couple of the century, throwing fundraisers and donating time to raising funds for city and state officials. Diana Praeliou could throw a barbecue in her backyard and rake in more than five hundred thousand dollars for charity. She was a mover and a shaker, and she made things happen. Every year Diana threw a Christmas party in their home for all Webster's family and friends. The guest list was over five hundred people. Every name on the list was someone of great importance, from the city and state politicians to the medical professionals associated with her husband's practice and every other scientist on his team from Bio One. They were all in attendance. No doubt, Webster and Diana Praeliou had the perfect life, she was the perfect wife, and he was the perfect husband. They were two souls that had joined together as man and wife in a union truly blessed by God. And in the past twenty years, there had been no man or woman who could come between them. How many women could say they were married to a neurosurgeon, a genius, a rich, handsome genius who happened to be on the cusp of a cure for Alzheimer's? Forget the money. They were rich beyond their wildest dreams, but then again, money meant nothing, they already had everything they wanted financially and materially, and most important, they had each other, and for the two of them, that was all that mattered.

Diana finished her ride with Rags, patted him down, told him what a good boy he was at least one hundred times, then called for Carlos on the walkie-talkie. Once in her bedroom, she began to undress as Rosa prepared her bath and turned on the plasma flat-screen hanging on the wall above the Jacuzzi. She put on a robe and walked into the wall-to-wall marble bathroom. She handed her robe to Rosa as Rosa held her hand and helped her sit down.

"Bien?" Rosa asked.

"Si, bien, Rosa. Gracias."

The Jacuzzi sat catty-corner under a large window with a perfect, picturesque view of the Arizona desert and Camelback Mountain. Several large saguaros, cactuses, and paloverdes lined the yard. There were scattered patches of red fairy dusters and desert willows and a few summer poppies strategically placed around the backyard. Arizona was truly the home of mother earth, and all the holistic benefits of the desert were there at Diana's fingertips. At forty-two years old, she looked as if she could pass for her late twenties or early thirties.

"Señora Praeliou, will you be eating downstairs today?" asked Rosa.

"No, I'll eat on the bedroom balcony. Bring the newspaper and the mail also," she ordered, before pressing a button and turning on the twenty-two-jet Jacuzzi.

Diana finished her bath and dressed in a cool tan-colored sweatsuit and white tee. Her toes were perfectly manicured, and she slipped on a pair of Bonjour Fleurette slippers and made her way to the balcony. A tray containing fresh fruit, toast, preserves, and freshly squeezed orange juice was waiting on the master bedroom balcony. She sat down, glanced at the headlines in today's *Arizona Capitol Times*, and then started to open the small pile of mail.

The envelope she held in her hand was handwritten, barely legible, foreign to her. She opened it and pulled out a folded sheet of yellow tablet paper. Small and large cut-out letters that had been pasted on the page read: "I know who you are, Daisy. Does your husband? Call this number, 602-555-3773, at 4:00 p.m. today or I call Webster!"

Large letters, small letters, red letters, black letters, white letters, all cut out and pasted on yellow tablet letter paper. She read it again, and again, and again as a horrible feeling of uncertainty fell on her shoulders like a heavy burden. It seemed as though someone was out there, watching her. *He called Webster by name. Oh, my God, what am I going to do?* She folded the note and put it back in the envelope.

"What am I going to do?"

"I am sorry, you talk to me, Señora?" asked Rosa, who was coming in to take the tray.

"Oh, my God, you startled me," said Diana. She had not realized Rosa was in the room behind her. "Rosa, please, some privacy for one moment."

"Do you need anything, Señora?"

"No, no, just a few minutes alone."

"Si, Señora," Rosa said, closing the bedroom door behind her.

Diana began to pace across the floor of the room. *What do they want? Why, why now, after all these years, why?* All those years of lying, pretending, and living a life that was a lie. She thought back to when she was younger, to all the mistakes of her past. She thought she had put them to rest, skeletons in a locked closet. She had paid her price and been given another chance at life. But now, all that was turning upside down, and her past was here, right here in her present. *Jesus, what am I going to do?* She had no options. The bottom line was that Webster could never, ever find out who she really was or any other sordid detail of her dirty, trifling life. Her secrets had to remain safe and unknown. It would ruin her marriage, ruin her life, and ruin everything. No, her secrets must never ever be exposed. She would do whatever had to be done to keep her past life a lie. She had to. She had no other choice. It was the only way to protect her husband, to protect their perfect life.

COCKTAIL TIME

Diana left her house at three-forty-five and went to the closest gas station where there was a pay phone. Whoever this person was, she didn't want him connected to her in any way. That meant she wasn't calling whoever it was from her house or her cell. She knew she had to think, and think smart. She wanted nothing more than to make sure that whoever this person was, he could never be traced back to her once this was over.

She parked her car, looked at her watch, and grabbed her purse. It cost fifty cents to make a pay phone call. She remembered the days it only cost a dime. She looked at the cut-and-paste note in her hand. It disgusted her that someone would even have the audacity to put her through this. Whatever it was he wanted she needed to know. Then she wanted him to be done with it. And if he even thought about coming back, then she would know she had a bigger problem. But first, she needed to find out exactly what this guy wanted.

She dialed the number, and a man's voice answered on the first ring.

"Hello, what do you want from me?" she asked, completely

frozen still at the thought of being blackmailed.

"I'm glad you don't want to beat around the bush. Let's just say I have video footage and photos of you doing what you do best." Nard chuckled as he spoke, just fucking with her.

"And why should I believe you," she asked.

"I can post it online for you, if you like, or just turn the bachelor party with you and your girlfriend into a DVD. Wow, I didn't know some of the shit you're doing was humanly possible, but somehow you managed, amazing, really amazing. One hundred thousand dollars, bitch. No more questions. You meet me in one hour at the Sleep Inn near the airport. Go into the back of the hotel and park next to the green Dumpster. And you better be there in one hour, alone, or the deal's off. Understood?"

"That's not enough time," she said calmly, recalling the night she and Trixie did a bachelor party for Sticks and were drugged with the date-rape drug, gamma-hydroxybutyrate, which the streets referred to as a mickey. Trixie never came back from it. That night, thanks to Daisy, messed her up for the rest of her life.

"You got plenty of time, go get the money out them safety deposit boxes you got and stop playing, before I go post your videos and photos on the Internet."

He knows a lot. How? How the hell does he know and how did he find me? Diana had thought that life was buried deep in the depths of her memory, but nothing is forgotten, and there's always tomorrow to remind you of yesterday.

"Hey, you hear me talking the fuck to you? One hour, you got that?" Nard asked one last time.

"One hour," Diana said, agreeing to the meet.

She hung up the phone and got back into her car, looking at her watch. *This is too much, this can't be happening,* she thought as tears began to roll down her cheeks.

She pulled into the Bank of America and hopped out of the car. She swung open one of the double glass doors and walked inside.

"Hi, Mrs. Praeliou."

She turned around and faced Inez, an assistant manager of the bank, who knew her well.

"Hi, Inez, can you please pull my safety deposit box for me?" asked Diana, not wanting to appear as if anything were wrong, even though she felt as if her world were crashing all around her. She took a deep breath, exhaling slowly, feeling as if she could barely finish her sentence.

"Of course, is everything all right?" asked Inez, feeling as if Ms. Praeliou wasn't herself.

"Oh, yes, just tired. That's all," Diana responded, feeling a wave of anxiety and a rush of adrenaline. *I just want this day to be over. I just want it over.* Little did she know, it was just beginning.

With less than thirty minutes of time and counting, she counted out a total of ten ten-thousand-dollar stacks from her personal safety deposit box for a whopping grand total of one hundred thousand.

A small price to pay for peace of mind. Thank God she had her own money. She was fortunate, she had hers, Webster had his, and then they had accounts and safety deposit boxes that they shared. She had her money already counted and bound before placing it in the box. She knew what she had, where she had it, and how much at all times. Diana Praeliou was a woman of great wealth, and her husband was ten times wealthier than she. Together they were the ultimate power couple, invincible, or so it seemed.

Nard watched as Daisy left the bank, hopped into her car, and headed for the highway. He followed several cars behind her just in case she was paranoid and watching to see if she was being followed. She pulled into the parking lot of the Sleep Inn and drove to the back. All the way to the left side of the lot, next to the hotel, was a green Dumpster, an empty parking spot beside it.

Great, now what? she thought to herself as she looked around the deserted parking lot. *What now? Just sit here. Maybe I'm to put the money in the Dumpster. Why would I do that, I want my photos and video. What if there isn't a video and there are no photos? What if this is just some asshole trying to get money from me? But then he wouldn't have called me Daisy.* Diana sat there, her mind scrambling, thought after thought, trying to put the situation into perspective. Fifteen minutes passed and the time was seven after four. Just as she was ready to start her car and drive off, her cell phone rang.

"Hello," she answered.

"Daisy, you got that?" the voice asked.

"Yes, I got it," she said, her heart sinking at the thought of this character invading her space and calling her cell phone. *How the hell does he have my number?*

"A'ight, come on, take the back door, you heard, and come up the stairwell to the second floor, room 215. And hurry up," the voice demanded before disconnecting.

Nard watched out the window as Daisy crossed the parking lot and took the back door as he had instructed, up to the second floor.

The door to the room was left cracked open, and as she approached it, she became nervous about what was waiting for her on the other side.

"Hello," she said as she pushed the door open.

The room was dark as night, not even the television was playing, so there was little light except that which played peekaboo through the drawn curtains.

Just as Diana stepped into the room, the door was pushed shut behind her, and a body approached her from the right side out of the bathroom doorway, quickly moving behind her, placing a gun to her side.

"Please don't kill me, I have the money," she whispered, scared to breathe as she began to feel faint, her heart pounding a mile a minute.

"Where is it?" Nard asked, wanting to see it for himself.

"Where are my pictures and my video you claim to have?"

Nard locked the hotel door as Diana held out the bag containing the money. "Here you go," she said.

"At least you do as you're told, but then again, you always did," said Nard as he pressed play on the video machine containing Sticks's homemade video special.

"Damn, how you got two dicks in your mouth like that is crazy. That is you, right?" he joked.

Daisy looked at herself as five men were gathered around her waiting for available parking space. Her friend, Trixie, had three other guys, and there were four more in another room that would have sex with the both of them. She remembered the next morning, waking up, realizing that she had had anal sex as well as group sex with a bunch of men Sticks had put her in the room with. She remembered feeling light-headed and knew she had been drugged, but she never remembered the night itself. Now she had it in living color, full view, no denying the reality of what she had felt the next morning, no questions needed to be asked. She watched as a man slid his penis in and out of her vagina while the others stood around in a circle over her waiting their turn for oral, anal, or vaginal sex, as if her body were nothing more than a Stop and Go.

"I've seen enough," she said, as if she was the one who could make demands.

"I haven't," said Nard, approaching her from behind completely naked. "Take off your clothes," Nard said as he took his hand, cupped her breast, and began to fondle her nipple.

"This wasn't part of the deal. You asked me to bring you the money and I did," she said as she pushed his hand off her.

"Bitch, I know you ain't got no problem letting a nigga fuck you. Look at them niggas," he said, pointing to the screen as Daisy was taking it three to one, and the cameraman was giving you an in-depth view, literally, of her ass. "You got to be kidding me. You're a fucking whore; take your clothes off and fold them neatly on the chair," he demanded. "Or do I got to make you?" he asked, pointing the gun at her head.

"You have to make me," she said, as a tear rolled down her cheek.

"If a gun to your head will make you feel better, bitch, then so fucking be it," Nard declared, forcing her down on her knees as he placed his dick in her mouth.

"Uh-uh, like the fucking video, bitch, suck it like you sucking that clown-ass nigga. Better, but you gonna get it right. Don't worry, Diana, we gonna find that Daisy girl, and I know she's in there somewhere."

"Daisy's been gone for twenty years now."

"Yeah, and so have I," he said sarcastically, Diana still not realizing who he was. "But don't worry, I'm gonna bring her back and fuck her real good, I know she likes getting fucked. Maybe you don't, but she does, ain't that right, Daisy?" asked Nard, grabbing her cheeks as he thrust himself up and down her throat, still standing above her. He came in her mouth, choking her as she tried not to swallow his semen. "Take it, swallow it, you know it's what you want."

She couldn't fight him, as he was too strong, his hands holding the sides of her face with so much force, he was able to stuff his penis down her throat and make her swallow it, still thrusting in and out of her mouth.

"Take it all, Daisy, take it just like you did in your movie."

A tear of frustration and anger rolled down her cheek, which she quickly wiped away. She refused to give him the satisfaction of knowing that he was getting at her. It seemed the more she resisted, the more he tried to hurt her, the more she pulled away, the more he forced himself harder. He pulled himself out of her, turning her around, and entered her from behind. His hands pulled at her hair as he stood on his feet, still forcing himself on her, but instead of her fighting, she spread her legs, opening herself so he could have his way. Hoping that it would all be over, that her secret would be safe and she could go home to her wonderful life, she lay there as he she felt him penetrating her anally, fucking her like an animal, purposely and forcefully stroking her, then vaginally, and again anally until he finally came in her rectum and collapsed on top of her.

She began to roll over to get off the bed. "Where do you think you're going?" said Nard as he grabbed her hair, smacked her face, and threw her back down on the bed.

"I'm not done with you yet," he said as he reached over to the nightstand, grabbed a prefilled needle, and stuck her in the arm. Within seconds she was out cold, her naked body lying peacefully still as he pulled out a video camera.

"This party's just getting started, Daisy, it's just getting started."

SAY GOOD-BYE, TERI

Diana woke up unable to move, her body frozen, her brain slowly transmitting images. The last thing she remembered was going to the bank, then driving. She looked around the hotel room and remembered him, forcing her and pointing a gun at her head.

Oh, God, if Webster ever finds out, please, God, just let this be over, just let this all be over. Diana could hardly move. Her body lay still as she tried to lift herself, too weak to hold herself up. She lay back down as thoughts of her life flashed before her. Thoughts of her husband, Webster, and the love they shared made her ball up into a fetal shape and wish she was never born. *How could this be happening to me? How does he know who I am?* She thought back to the day that Webster proposed. He had called suddenly, as if he was prepared to stop time. He told her to be ready, and he picked her up from a job she had gotten at a social services clinic after graduating from Arizona State.

"Where are we going?" she asked, not caring if he took her to the end of earth or Satan's dungeon. Wherever he wanted to be with her, she would go. She had fallen in love with Webster and would do anything for him.

Only Webster would have a helicopter waiting for them, and just like that, he whisked her away in the sky, flew her above Phoenix as a helicopter flew by them and began to write in the sky, "I love you, Diana, will you marry me?" for all of Phoenix and Scottsdale to see. She looked out the window of the helicopter and there in big fluffy clouds she read her proposal in the sky.

"Yes, Webster, yes, I'll marry you," she said as she hugged him tightly. Never having any second thoughts, the two of them had a small wedding, with her college friend Paige serving as her bridesmaid, and Webster's closest friend from high school serving as his best man.

The ceremony was held in Vegas at the Bellagio in 1992. They had been married for the past fourteen years and still, to this day, Diana loved Webster just as she had when they were college sweethearts. And even though they never had children, it didn't matter. It wasn't that they didn't want children, they tried many times, and each and every time, Diana lost the baby due to miscarriage. They realized that children were out of the question after Diana suffered three miscarriages in a row.

"It's okay, we don't need children to be a family, Diana. You are all the family I will ever need," whispered Webster in Diana's ear as he walked her to the front door of their beautiful home facing Camelback Mountain.

"I love you, Webster, you are the best husband in the whole world." Diana smiled as he held her tightly.

"I love you, too," he whispered back to her. "And just to show you how much I love you, I got you something," he said, hoping the news of a gift would cheer her spirit.

"What? Please tell me, what is it?" she begged to know, not wanting for anything.

"Look outside," said Webster, pointing to the newborn colt grazing in the backyard.

"Webster, it's a horse," she said confusedly.

"Not just a horse, a stallion, a true Thoroughbred, and he's yours, all yours. You can raise him, and race him, if you like." Webster smiled, hoping that she would approve, and she did, she most certainly did.

The colt was the gift of life from her husband, letting her know that everything would be okay, even though she had lost their third baby and the doctors said she would never carry or possibly even conceive again, and she never did. But having no children didn't change the love, it changed nothing, only made them closer, stronger, and even more a family, because each was all the other had in the world.

Oh, my God, how long have I been here? she thought to herself as she looked around the hotel room. The shades were drawn and the room was dark. She rolled over in the bed, her body feeling heavy, her head pounding, and her vision a tad blurry.

Webster! I have to hurry home, I have to go. She tried to lift her body but was unable to, and not only did a sudden feeling of nausea come over her, but the room started spinning out of control, and she felt as if she was suffering from a horrific case of vertigo. Her balance, her vision, her splitting head, and her nausea consumed her. *If only I could throw up and make it all go away,* she thought, wishing she could erase whatever drug was in her system. *Please, God, just let me get home, just let me get home.*

Her ravaged body smelled of sex and the sex of another man consumed even herself. *I can't go home like this. Look at me.* She sat on the edge of the bed, facing an oblong mirror above a desk and for a split second, she didn't even recognize herself. Her makeup was worn and stained, her hair wild and matted, her facial muscles still twisted from the drug. Her sensory and motor skills were turned off, completely. She moved like a drunk on Vicodin. *Get it together. Come on, let's get out of here,* she told herself, wiping her eyes as she walked, using the wall for support, into the bathroom. She clicked on the light, "Oh, no," she said, blinded by the light, before clicking the switch downward and turning the lights off.

Her body somewhat sore, she sat on the edge of the toilet seat and turned on the shower. Then, carefully, she stepped into the tub, holding on to the wall, careful not to slip and fall. Diana moved as close to the shower of water as she could, resting her body against the tiled wall. The water beat down on her body and rolled down the drain along with all the evidence of the nightmare she had encountered.

She tried to remember what day she had come to the hotel and what day it could be, but she couldn't. All she did know was that Webster was sure to be looking for her, probably calling the police and filing a missing persons report by now. *How the hell am I going to drive?* Where there is a will there is a way, and if one person could find the will to get herself home, safe and sound, it would be Diana.

Nard sat in his bedroom on the floor, his television playing the Channel 3 *Eyewitness News*. Once again, he had collected a few magazines and newspapers and was going through them, cutting and clipping what he needed.

"Nard, what the hell are you doing? Look at this mess," said Beverly, sounding as if he were thirteen instead of forty-two. I know you don't think I'm cleaning this up. I'm not," Beverly said heatedly.

"I got it, I got it, no worries," he said, rehashing slang he had picked up from his young guns that ran the block for Liddles.

"Yeah, I'ma be worried all right, worried about you running around the way you do."

"Relax, everything is fine. You don't need to worry about me, I'm building my house right now, Liddles got the workers, the materials, and once it's fixed up, you can come and visit me, but you don't have to worry. I'm okay," said Nard, shaking his head. "I'm gonna be okay."

"All right, well, hurry up. I need your help 'cause I had to send Tyrone to the liquor store. Everybody is gonna be here any minute now for Thanksgiving dinner. Everybody's coming 'cause it's your first holiday back home. Rev and Maeleen, Donna and her new boyfriend, Carl, Mia and Dayanna, and I even invited Chris. You know, your cousin stopped getting high and is working for a meat distributor down in South Philly. Who would have ever thought he would get himself together? It should be a real nice holiday, and the best part is you're home, baby, after all these years, my baby is home."

Beverly bent down, held Nard's face, and kissed his forehead.

"That food sure does smell good."

"You know I makes it do what it do, baby," she teased, sounding like Jamie Foxx as she closed the door behind her.

Diana, with nothing but a prayer on her back, opened the door to the hotel room. A Spanish woman was cleaning the room next door.

"Buenos días, Señora."

"Buenos días," she responded.

Diana slipped out of the Sleep Inn and slowly walked over to her car, parked next to the large green Dumpster. The key was in her pocketbook, which she fumbled after, putting on a pair of oversized sunglasses to hide from the light. Once inside the car she realized the day of the week and how long she had been missing. Today would be the second day in a row she had not been home. Four o'clock this afternoon would make a complete forty-eight hours. She looked at the time. It was eleven-thirty-three in the morning.

Maybe had she turned on the news before she left the hotel, or even the car radio, she would have heard the special news bulletin or seen her face spread all over the television screen. But she hadn't. Diana Poitier Praeliou was the headline story for every news station, including CNN.

Webster Praeliou had been shot and killed while having sex with an unidentified woman. His penis was still inside the woman's vagina at the time the bodies were found. The police reported both Webster Praeliou and the unidentified woman were found with two gunshot wounds to the head.

The gun used in the murder was found outside in a Dumpster behind the hotel of the crime scene. The police would later identify the woman as Paige Hunter, Diana's best friend and college roommate. Paige and Webster had been having an affair for the past nine months.

It turned out that Webster had never left town, nor did he plan to. His conference in Miami had actually been postponed, but he failed to mention that. Instead, he pretended to be traveling. He packed a carry-on bag and went twenty minutes away from his home to downtown Phoenix, where he checked in to a hotel with Paige.

After housekeeping found the bodies, the hotel manager phoned 911. Of course, the police were on the scene within seconds, combing the hotel and surrounding area looking for clues, and they found the gun immediately. Within a matter of hours, forensics came back with fingerprints on the gun belonging to none other than Diana Praeliou, Webster's wife. An arrest warrant for Diana was issued, and an all-points bulletin alert was sent out as well.

As Diana turned the corner that led to her block, on Camelback Mountain, she could see the red and blue lights atop a crowd of police cars that were surrounding her home.

Jesus, Webster, you had to file a missing persons report, didn't you? I knew he'd do this. Diana knew her husband all too well, and there was no way she could be missing without his calling in the army and the national guard.

She parked her car down the street in the closest available parking space, not wanting to intrude on all the police vehicles and the commotion on her lawn. She locked her car and walked up the block to the front of the house.

"Sorry, ma'am, no one allowed except for authorized personnel," said an officer.

"I live here... what's going on?"

"Are you Diana Praeliou?"

"Yes, I am Diana Praeliou. This is my house and I live here. Did my husband call you?"

"Diana Praeliou, you're under arrest. Please turn around and place your hands behind your back," the officer said as he stepped back from her and drew his automatic, pointing it at her face.

"Arrest for what?"

"For the murder of Webster Praeliou and Paige Hunter," said the officer as he manhandled Diana, taking her into custody as the other officers ran over to where the arrest was being made on her front lawn.

"Are you joking? You must be mistaken," she said matter-of-factly. She felt her world begin to shatter as the officer handcuffed her, tears running down her cheeks as thoughts of her husband, Webster, being murdered crippled her into a mini-meltdown.

"No," she screamed. "No, not Webster. No, please, God, no."

ONE WEEK LATER

Lieutenant Delgado was parked outside Graterford Prison waiting for his brother Sammy to come walking through the gates. Tommy had been sitting there since six-thirty. He could only imagine spending nine years behind bars, only to be released and find no one waiting for you. He wanted to be there. They started releases as early as five-thirty, so he could walk out the door at any moment. It had been a long time since he had seen his kid brother—nineteen years, five months, and three days to be exact. Nineteen years is a long time, but then again, he had served his time straight for robbing a Brinks truck. He refused parole. He could have come home after serving thirteen years, but the family didn't want the cops sniffing around, so Tommy wrote him and told him to stay inside, and he did, for another six years. No one visited, least of all Tommy. God forbid someone that he had arrested see him in the visiting room. That would only have made life harder for Sammy. Not that life was hard. Sammy was making more money on the inside than one could have imagined.

Tommy looked at the reflection of himself in the mirror. He had done a lot, seen a lot, and lived a lot of lives. He turned his face to the side. The lines of age, frustration, and stress had begun to set in. *Shit, I'll be fifty in two more weeks. I look good, though, I'm still here, God bless the dead.*

He turned his face to the other side and stroked his jaw. He needed a shave; he could feel the stubble. He smiled at himself. *You've had a great life, Tommy Delgado, a great life.* And he had, because Tommy had family, a network unlike any other. It crossed states, and his family was tied into other families. Knowing that there was a sea of men ready to stand strong and battle for any cause made life's turbulent ups and downs worth it. Plus, his family had honor, and that was something that would last forever and stays with you always, and he had honor among men.

"Whadda ya doing?" asked a gray-haired, rail-thin Sammy, puffing on a Newport as he leaned down and looked at his brother admiring himself in the mirror. "You think you're sexy? Jesus Christ, open the door, Mr. America?" he joked.

"Sammy, oh, my God, look at you." Tommy smiled, happy to see his kid brother, a mirror image of himself. He opened the driver's-side car door and got out of the car, making his way around the back of the car to hug his brother. "Jesus Christ, Sammy, look at your hair, it's so gray."

"Do you believe this shit?" he said, as if he couldn't stand it. "I gotta get my hair done," he said, hugging his brother.

"You sound like a woman," joked Tommy.

"You look like one," joked Sammy back.

"It's good to see you," said Tommy, smiling.

"It's good to see you, too." Sammy smiled, "Where's that FBI ex-wife of yours?" he said, looking all around as if the police were scoping him out.

"Please don't say her fucking name, it's like saying beetle juice. This bitch used to come with her unit, Jesus Christ," said Tommy opening his door, "and the fucking ATF, DEA, and every other agency," he continued, sitting behind the wheel as Sammy closed his door, "this psychotic bitch could think of just to get her child support or a document signed. I don't know where she is and I don't want to know. She doesn't bother me anymore and I don't bother her. I think we have a mutual hate relationship, built on mutual disrespect and disregard for one another, and it works, you know?"

"No, I really don't know," said Sammy, still a tad upset with Viv for arresting him. But had his brother not been such a shithead to her, she probably would have let him go. Sammy was glad he didn't have the women problems Tommy always had. He had married his childhood sweetheart and they were still together. Of course, Sammy did what he wanted to throughout his life, but he always loved Marie, and he always took care of her. What was Marie going to do? She had had five babies within eight years, locking herself to him for the rest of their lives. Right now, she was waiting for him at their house, with their children and grandchildren. And later tonight at the Donatella Lounge on the corner of Ninth and Snyder, they would join everyone from the family to celebrate Sammy's homecoming.

Nothing but the finest meats, lobsters, and champagne was being sent in for Sammy, and right now everyone who mattered in South Philly was preparing for his homecoming. It would be a night that no one would ever forget. Since Tommy was an officer of the law, he would have to sit that party out. Tommy had big plans, and someday he would be the chief of police, and he would do whatever it took to make that happen. And it would, one day, of course. But there was nothing he wouldn't do for Sammy and nothing he wouldn't do to protect the family.

"I need you to take me to the house on Livezly Lane. Remember the house?" asked Sammy.

"Yeah," said Tommy, looking quite confused.

"Well, I'm gonna need your help," said Sammy. "And we got to grab some shovels, too."

Tommy heard the word "shovels" and automatically responded as if the last thing he was doing was digging holes to bury god knows who for Sammy.

"Shovels, what the hell you want to do with a shovel?" he asked, not sure he even wanted to hear it. "I'm a fucking lieutenant, Sammy, come on. I can't fuck around with you, and no bullshit, you hear me?"

"We can stop at Home Depot, get the shovels, then go to Livezly Lane," said Sammy with a devious grin on his face.

"What do we need shovels for and what's at Livezly Lane?" demanded Tommy.

"I got so much money buried in my old backyard, Tommy. I swear to God, at least a million dollars buried out there."

"Are you fucking kidding me, Sammy?"

"Would I fucking lie to you?" Sammy asked, looking at his brother as if Tommy were fresh out of the looney bin for even assuming he was joking.

"Come on, you gotta help me. All you got to do is pull that badge out on whoever's living there and we're digging up the backyard. Come on, what are you a cop for? I got shit to do, I got a party tonight, baby. How do I look?" Sammy asked in all seriousness. "I look good, right, Tommy?"

"You look like a million bucks, Sammy, a million bucks."

"Ha, good answer." Sammy laughed as he grabbed his older brother around the neck. "Good fucking answer."

Daisy went back to her block after seeing her assigned social worker. She felt as if she were trapped in a nightmare not her own. The past week spent behind bars had been pure hell. She never thought in a million years she would ever be living her life without Webster, let alone that she would be charged with murdering him. She passed the guard's desk on her block just as a CO held out her mail and passed it to her.

In this facility, mail was opened and screened before being given to the inmates. Diana was hoping that she would receive a letter from her lawyer with good news. She had requested another bail hearing because her bail had been denied. Her lawyer was hopeful, but it didn't look as if she'd be granted another hearing. With Diana's DNA evidence found at the scene of the crime and prints on the murder weapon, it didn't appear that she would be going anywhere, but rather that she'd be spending the rest of her life behind bars, and there was nothing anyone could do to change that.

She looked at the first envelope and then the second. Her heart began to pound, as her fingers and her hand began trembling. She recognized the writing and realized it was that of the blackmailer, as the envelope looked identical to the first one she had received from him. Quickly, she walked back down the block, careful not to let anyone see what she was holding. She went into her cell, sat down on the edge of the bottom bunk, and pulled out the letter inside. It was him, the same person. She could tell by the cut-and-paste letters scattered across the lined yellow tablet paper. The note was barely readable. She slowly made out the cut-and-paste wordplay, and it was then that she realized exactly who had blackmailed her, killed her cousin, and brutally murdered her husband. And as she read the note, twenty years of pieces of a puzzle slowly came together in her mind, and she knew who he was.

"Hope You Got An Alibi—You're Gonna Need One, Bitch!"

ABOUT THE AUTHOR

Teri Woods is a native of Philadelphia. She worked as a legal secretary/paralegal for eight years in a Philadelphia Center City law firm. She began writing her first book, *True to the Game*, in 1992 and began to submit her work to publishers. After being turned down, the book sat dormant in a closet for four years. In 1998, she began selling handmade copies of the book out of the trunk of her car. With the success of the handmade books, she started her own publishing and production company, Teri Woods Publishing.

Teri Woods has successfully written, co-authored, and published twenty-one novels and sold over two million copies worldwide. She is currently working on her next release.

For more information visit www.teriwoodspublishing.com

CPSIA information can be obtained at www.ICGtesting.com
Printed in the USA
LVOW131429010513

331842LV00001B/153/P